Other Books by Terah Edun

COURTLIGHT SERIES

SWORN TO RAISE (Book One)

SWORN TO TRANSFER (Book Two)

SWORN TO CONFLICT (Book Three)

SWORN TO SECRECY (Book Four)

SWORN TO DEFIANCE (Book Five)

SWORN TO ASCENSION (Book Six)*

CROWN SERVICE SERIES

BLADES OF MAGIC (Book One)

BLADES OF ILLUSION (Book Two)*

SARATH WEB SERIES

ACCESSION (Book One)

INHERITANCE (Book Two)*

*Forthcoming

Want to get an email when my next book is released?

Sign up here: bit.ly/SubscribetoTerahsNewsletter

THE SARATH WEB SERIES

BOOK ONE

accession

TERAH EDUN

CHAPTER ONE

Half-blinded by the stinging wind as she lugged a paintball gun at her side and ducked for cover behind a rather large oak tree, Katherine Thompson promised herself this was the *last* time she would agree to go on a double-date with her sister Rose. She didn't care if the entire football team showed up and promised her everlasting love, either. Her feet hurt from the too-tight boots Rose had forced on her from her mammoth closet, her face stung from what she thought was poison ivy, and the linebacker who was her date was taking vicious glee in aiming agonizing balls of bright yellow paint at her butt.

"Katherine!" she heard her sister shout from a distance.

Katherine grimaced. She was hunkered down by the tree and didn't want to give up her position. Besides, where had Rose been for the last half-hour while she was being chased down like a deer in hunting season?

"Probably off with her tongue down Derrick's throat for the umpteenth time," she grumbled as a sharp wind hit her in the face.

It was the middle of winter and *cold*—cold for Georgia, that is. Probably no less than fifty degrees with the wind chill. But still her face felt like she was getting frostbite and her hands were so stiff that she wasn't sure that she could put down the paintball gun even if she wanted to. Katherine knew she had two options to end this game. Come out, let the idiot date whose name she had forgotten mow her down, and surrender. *Or* find Rose and Derrick, because of course the two lovers on opposite teams were hunkered down together, and end this once and for all. One was easy. The other harder.

Palming her loaded gun, she snuck off with a smirk. No one ever accused Katherine Thompson of taking the easy route. Besides, Rose deserved a little unpleasantness once in a while. She was beautiful, she was smart, and she would be the Queen of Sandersville one day. For once Katherine wanted to win something. And pelting her sister's boyfriend with painful green balls of splat seemed just the thing to cure her misery. He was a jerk anyway. She really couldn't see what Rose saw in him.

She knew what she saw—a broad-shouldered idiot with scraggly, wheat-colored hair and eyes that reminded her of a Labrador retriever's. Too stupid to know he *was* stupid. Unfortunately, Derrick came from one of the most powerful families in Lancashire County, was a warlock in his own right, and happened to be smitten with Rose. All of which shown like "warning, collision ahead" signs on a highway, that Katherine would eventually be calling the idiot her brother-in-law.

 2

As she sprinted around large boulders, keeping low to the ground, she heard the *snap* of a branch off to her left. She paused. And then a second branch snapped, followed by a giggle shortly after. She smiled. She had them. The sound was coming from the weeping willow just to the west. It was a tree that Katherine knew well from childhood. She and Rose had played around the old grandmother tree and in the hidden nook inside the branches all the time. As she sprinted forward in cautious bounds, she almost cackled. There was only one way in and one way out of Rose's new lover's nook. As Katherine got to the willow's roots that sprawled above ground in gigantic arcs, she slowed down, wary of spooking them. But she heard no noise. Made no sounds as she crept forward.

And then it was confirmed. Voices echoed from the nook—she'd found her sister alongside her rat of a boyfriend.

"She must be halfway across the course. Or she would have come when I called," whispered Rose.

"Why did you bring her?" Derrick complained in response.

"She's my little sister and she needed to get out of the house. Always cooped up in her room with those old spell books."

"She's so weird. If she's not off communing with trees in the dead of night, she's studying with that crazy friend of hers," snorted Derrick.

Katherine heard Rose shift around as she waited for her to say something. Anything.

"She's all right," Rose said defensively.

"I just meant the girl couldn't get a date on her own. I had to *beg* Mark to take her on."

"Well, you got him here. That's all that matters," said Rose. "Now let's get back to why *we're* here."

3

Shuffles in the branches made Katherine certain they were back to kissing. She felt her resentment grow. She hadn't wanted to come. Rose had begged *her* to go with them because their mother wouldn't let Rose go out alone without a chaperone. Katherine, although younger than Rose by two years, qualified. Katherine knew that her mother hated Derrick just as much as she did. It took a lot of convincing to let her daughter and heir go off with the imbecile, as Mother scathingly referred to him in private, and the only reason Derrick was still around was because the alliance between their families had been written into the concord long before Rose and Derrick had been born.

The prophecy also happened to be the only reason Rose had her given name. Mockingly, Katherine quoted the lines in her head, *Star-crossed lovers and all that shall be born, from Lancashire County the Rose and the Thorn shall rule, blah blah blah.* Even her mother wasn't so disgusted with Derrick that she would tempt fate like that. The three wise sisters didn't take kindly to lowly witches, or even *queens*, who thought that they were above their premonitions.

With a battle cry, Katherine surged out of her hiding spot, khakis covered in yellow paint and firing at random. The shrieks of Rose met her as she and her boyfriend jumped apart from their lip-lock. Derrick shouted and threw up a shield with his hands. And then the tables turned.

As powerful as Katherine was stubborn, Rose commanded the vines on the ground around them to lock onto Katherine's boots. With a vicious twist of her hand, her younger sister was strung up in the tree by her feet. To Katherine's credit, she didn't drop the paintball gun or stop firing. But it didn't matter, because the vines around her feet had her body facing out of the alcove. She heard the humiliating, gut-wrenching laughter of Derrick behind her as he watched her swing by her heels.

"Put me down!"

"You little brat!" shrieked Rose at the same time.

"Rose, this is so not fair! We said powers are off limits!"

Rose came rushing around so that Katherine could see her from where she hung upside down. Ignoring her sister's complaint, she poked Katherine in her vested stomach with a furious finger. "Did you really think you could surprise your *queen*?"

"*Future* queen," spat out Katherine in irritation.

Rose sniffed. "Whatever, I've always been more powerful than you. There was no way you could have landed a finger on me."

"No, you're just able to *use* your powers," growled Katherine.

"Semantics," said Rose in a huff.

"I don't even think you know what that means," retorted Katherine.

"Babe," whined her boyfriend at the same time, "this little brat needs a lesson."

"If you could teach me anything, it would be on how to be an idiot," muttered Katherine disdainfully.

"What did you say, you little brat?" demanded an outraged Derrick.

"I said someone who's only two years older than me has gotten too big for his britches."

Then Katherine paused. "Oh wait, that's not it."

"That's right," grunted the boy-Labrador retriever from somewhere behind her. He thought he had won. That she was recanting her statement. Oh no. Not Katherine.

5

A wicked smile crossed Katherine's face. Even though she still hung upside down by her ankles and blood was rushing to her head.

"Yes," Katherine said smugly. "You're too much an idiot to think you're more powerful than me. You just assume that because you're going to be banging the queen-to-be, you'll outrank me. Fool. Never in a million years. You'll always be a Labrador."

That was Katherine for you. She never knew when to leave well enough alone. And, when in a hole, how *not* to dig herself deeper.

Fortunately, she couldn't say much more to make the situation worse. She looked up at her sister Rose who had turned an interesting shade of red.

Although Katherine wasn't sure if Rose was beet-red because of embarrassment or anger. But Katherine was guessing anger; Rose wasn't a blushing bride to be shocked by a little hint of sex. Instead, she was usually an uptight bitch who wouldn't let an insult slide. From anyone. Not even family.

Katherine knew that and she had deliberately played with Rose's emotions. Hoping to invoke a response that would make Rose so angry that her powers wouldn't work. After all, it required focus to call on the elements, and if there was one thing that Katherine could count on, it was that her airheaded sister wouldn't be able to focus on the manipulation of the land and trees around them for more than five minutes.

Heaven help her when she took the throne and needed to command the forest for the defense of the town.

Of course, that'll probably never happen, Katherine thought wryly. She couldn't remember the last time the Queen of

 6

Sandersville had been called on to do more than trap a rabid wolf in a thicket grove, much less take on invaders.

Snapping back to focusing on her sister, Katherine realized with dismay that Rose's anger wasn't loosening her concentration. Instead, it focused it. Katherine could feel the vines only growing tighter around her ankles. She knew she was going to have livid bruises tomorrow.

Rats, thought Katherine. *Time for Plan B.*

Although she hated to do it, she tried to be nice. If you couldn't kill your flies with vinegar and a fly-swatter, honey and luring them into a trap was the next-best step.

"Look, I'm sorry. Really. Can we let it go?," Katherine said in a sugary-sweet tone that didn't quite disguise the disgust in her voice.

She didn't hate Rose. Really, she didn't. She also didn't hate the Labrador. At some point in the last year, she had reconciled herself to the notion that those two idiots were the future rulers of her hometown. But that didn't mean Katherine was crazy about the idea. Democracy be damned. She just didn't want to have to bow and scrape to two idiots who weren't fit to run a brothel, much less a small town of over a thousand families.

But it didn't really matter what she wanted. Not right now. Besides, if her sister didn't inherit the throne, then she would. And she certainly didn't want the throne for herself.

She wanted *out*. She wanted out of this small town. She wanted out of this restrictive old-world covenant of a land ruled by witches, warlocks, and queens. She didn't know where she would go, but she certainly knew when. Like all teens, she lived under her mother's roof and under the rule of the local queen (also her mother) until she was eighteen and chose to leave.

Eighteen was a long and hard two years down the road. And she had to live with the would-be queen-from-hell until that time. If she couldn't speak her mind about it now, then when could she?

So Katherine put in her hits and angered Rose when she could. Because when Rose became her queen, her word really would be law.

Still, Katherine knew she was beat now. Slumping her shoulders as she tried to ease up the weight of her body while pushing up from the ground with her hands, Katherine tried another tactic. Firm resolution.

With a hint of a whine in her furious tone, Katherine said, "Put me down."

There was only a hint of weakness in her tone. She refused to cry in front of her domineering older sister. Rose might be the future Queen of Sandersville, Georgia, literally and figuratively, with all the responsibilities that came with that—including protecting her people. But she was just as much as a bitch as the rest of the coven heirs—the female and male young elite who would one day inherit their parents' seats on the coven council as well as their tiny stretch of domain in the southern plantation-dotted land they called home.

Rose leaned forward and said with great pleasure, "I don't think so. I rather like you up there."

Katherine watched a smirk cross Rose's face one more time. And then she dropped her gun and clocked her sister hard in the nose.

Rose hadn't expected that. Fighting like a human was so gauche. She fell screaming to the dirt with blood streaming from her pretty, freckle-free nose.

Katherine didn't have long to savor her win.

They made her pay.

 8

CHAPTER TWO

Derrick walked around until he stood just behind Rose's right shoulder and glared menacingly. Or at least he gave what Katherine was convinced he thought was a menacing look. Katherine thought he looked like a constipated golden retriever, but she wasn't going to tell him that. Uninspiring façade or not, Derrick was a perfectly adept warlock, according to the standards of their small town. His powers were even considered *dangerous*. You know, for a small town, that is.

On a scale of one to ten, Katherine thought of him as a level two, right above the ferocious might of a shih-tzu and below a cockapoo. She didn't think of herself in dog terms, but all humor aside, she knew that she herself was closer to a twelve. But she couldn't tell them that or use her own gifts to *prove* that.

You know the old saying 'If I tell you, I'll have to kill you?' Katherine thought wryly while she waited for her sister and Derrick to do their worst. *Well, I have the opposite problem. If I show you my gifts, you'll be dead. There's no explaining, no second guessing.* Which was why even though she was furious with her older sister, she couldn't defend herself. Not as a witch. Katherine might not *like* her sister, but she loved her. Loved her in the way that siblings that fought like cats and dogs, but still hung together against a common enemy did. Since they were rarely on the same side of *anything* recently, Rose and Katherine had yet to face anything worse than the schoolyard bully they had taken down together when Katherine was in kindergarten and Rose was in second grade. That incident had proved that blood trumped friends, at least in the all-out war over the marbles container, that is.

But now? Now, Rose and I never really see eye-to-eye at all, Katherine thought with a shiver. *She must have been desperate to invite me on this stupid escapade. I know I was pretty stupid to accept the invitation. And now I'm going to pay for that. That hope that for* once *Rose wanted me along for me, as her sister...as a friend.*

Then Derrick called in his powers as a warlock gifted with domain over the wind and the weather, and she had no more time to think about what could have been. Only what was to come. They wouldn't kill her. Rose wasn't evil. But she wasn't above scaring her sister mentally and leaving a few scars physically. She wouldn't be a future queen if she wasn't a little bit callous. Small town or no. Katherine gulped. This far up in the air, she couldn't call on the small amount of talent she was willing to use, let alone best her sister and her sister's boyfriend at their own game. But only because she didn't want to kill her only sister...yet.

Derrick began to twirl his finger in the air just in front of Katherine's nose. Slowly at first. But faster and faster as time went on. As his finger moved so did her body, until she was twirling around like a spinning top on a fishing line.

Before Katherine's mind started to get disoriented she thought, *He might only be a level two, but even a two can be dangerous if they use their gifts correctly.*

It was a lesson she would remember for the rest of her life. But in that moment, all she wanted to do was hurl.

Derrick kept up on twirling her around and around in the air for five minutes. It felt like a lifetime.

With a callous laugh, Rose left with Derrick some time later. Katherine didn't know when, because the spinning continued long after they left. She wasn't ashamed to say that she threw up in her mouth. Once the spinning finally stopped, she tried to wipe away the bitter taste of the bile unsuccessfully while struggling to hold back her fury.

She had to. She knew what would happen if she didn't: a maelstrom a lot worse than Derrick's wind trick would tear through the woods and she wouldn't be able to stop it.

"Deep breaths," she told herself as she fought to calm down.

Five minutes later, she gingerly reached out to the spirit of the forest. Asking for its help in freeing herself from her bondage would mean she didn't have to call on her own gifts.

She soon gave up. It was clear from the emptiness around her that the spirit either wasn't listening or didn't care to hear the pleas of a witch who had set fire to an acre of its land just last week. So she did it the old-fashioned way.

She began to swing her body back and forth. Rocking faster and faster as she lunged each time higher and higher. She was trying to grab hold of her legs. It *felt* like she was doing crunches from hell. Two tries later, a triumphant, "Got it!" rang out.

Slowly climbing up her own body while upside down she managed to fish out the knife she'd hidden in the pinching boots, her only saving grace. Then she hacked away at the vines with a whispered, "Sorry," to the spirit of the old willow they belonged to. The vines binding her finally snapped and she fell to the ground.

"So much for sisterly bonding," she said as she stood up with an aching butt and dusting dirt off her bum.

She started to walk out into the setting sun, then she remembered the paintball gun lying forlornly in the dirt. Gripping it while pocketing the knife, she darted through the forest. She had no doubt they'd all left her behind. But the great thing about living in a small town was that nothing was too far from anything else.

Besides, she knew these woods like the back of her hand.

It took her an hour to hike from the forest to the one highway that ran into town and another twenty minutes to trot quickly across the bridge stretching through the gorge and reach the main part of town. But home was a further five miles across town. When she limped into the local bar looking for water, a chorus of "Katy-girl" met her at the door. She looked up to see Boris and Sam manning the bar at their usual stations. They toasted her with their half-consumed bottles of beer.

With stiff legs she walked to the bar and leaned on the counter.

"Trip," she groaned aloud, "I'm dying."

The diminutive bartender, a gnome and excellent brew master, gave her a wry glance. "Up in the forests again."

"Yes, but not for what you think."

"Really now?" said Trip while pulling on a tap for sparkling water—her favorite.

Gratefully she accepted his offering and swallowed the first gulp to say glumly, "Really, I wish I *had* been aura-gazing. Rose stranded me in the forest. Again."

Trip shook his head in distaste. "That girl really needs to learn that a queen first serves. She canna rule without it."

His thick Irish brogue was showing through.

"It's what I've been telling her for years," said Katherine eagerly. Out of all the townspeople, Trip was one of the few that didn't worship the ground her sister—and for that matter, her mother—walked on.

He shook his towel at her. "Well, tell her harder. Now off with you. Young ladies don't belong in bars."

"If I can stand on my own two feet I belong here," she countered. She hated that. By witch standards she was old enough to order hensbane, a toxic plant so lethal it was a Level 5 coven-controlled substance. So standing in a liquor-serving bar was child's play.

He sighed. "Aye, lass, but for tonight it is not your place. Now go home—your mum will be worried."

She nodded and turned to limp off. From behind her she heard Trip call out, "Ryan, take Katy-girl home!"

She turned to protest that she didn't *need* the police captain's help, but he had already eagerly accepted.

As she looked up into Ryan Moning's face, she glared. He shrugged on his coat and held the door open for her. Katherine had known since she was five that the man had a crush on her mother. She knew because she had started reading auras like road maps when she'd encountered her first crush in grade school.

That same crush had pushed her into a pond and laughed. But not for long. She smiled at the memory of his feet freezing in the shallow water. He had been stuck for hours. After that little push of power from her, he had left her alone, and she had considered them even. But she held the grudge against Moning still because it was just gross. Hell, her father had still been alive then!

Sighing, she got into the passenger's side of the town's police car and irritably stared out the window at the passing buildings—the town hall, the main library, the fireman's station, until finally nothing but trees met her gaze. Firmly she ignored his attempts at starting a conversation until they came to the gates of the queen's house.

Quickly she opened the door when the car stopped. "I can make my way from here, thanks for the ride!"

As he was protesting, she slammed the door and hustled through the wrought-iron gates.

She didn't bother turning around as she limped forward in her dirty jeans, carrying the paintball gun. She knew he was still there. Once his headlights had fully receded into the dusk, she was able to relax.

Night had fallen. The moon shone as it rose in the sky and she walked the mile-long driveway in perfect contentment. This was her domain. The outside. The clean air. The night sky.

As she reached the door, which swung open without a touch, Katherine wondered what excuse Rose had given their mother this time.

No servants met her at the door. They didn't have any. Her mother insisted on doing everything themselves, or magically, if possible. Everyone was responsible for their own mess. Which was all fine and dandy, but Katherine didn't have the domestic powers that most of her family did. The one time she'd tried to fold the laundry with a wave of her hand, she had ended up bursting the water pipes *and* setting the carpet on fire. Her magic was different. Darker. Which was why she did her best to never use it. So while Rose and the queen were away on town duties, it was Katherine that ended up washing her own clothes, folding laundry, scrubbing the toilet, and picking pet dander out of the carpet.

As she walked into a sparkling home, she knew her mother had spent the afternoon cleaning. Which meant she'd waved her finger and wiped all the dust away, twitched her hand and dispelled the odor as well as the grime, and waved her arm to straighten all of the furniture.

It was good to be queen.

As she dropped her bag and her gun at the foot of the staircase, she yelled for her mom. "Mother!"

"In the kitchen!"

Taking off the paintball vest, as well, she dropped it with the other stuff.

"Mother, Rose—" Katherine complained, but stopped short.

Because when she entered the kitchen two things met her senses: the smell of cinnamon buns fresh from the oven, and the smirk of her sister leaning against the counter in a fresh new outfit with ribbons in her hair and not a smidgen of blood on her.

Katherine glared and said shortly, "Rose trapped me in the forest and took off with Derrick and his friend."

Rose quickly snapped her head over to her mother who was busy bending over the stove. "What Katy didn't tell you was that she deliberately sabotaged me. We were supposed to be a team!"

"Team," Katherine gasped. "You were too busy with your tongue stuck down that idiot's throat to realize the meaning of the word 'team.'"

"Girls!" snapped their mother as she turned around and tossed her apron in the closet. "Inside and *sisterly* voices, please."

Eyeing Katherine, she continued, "Katy, go upstairs and get cleaned up. Dinner's almost ready."

Katherine stared at her mother with her mouth hanging open. "What about her?"

"She's already clean."

"I mean what are you going to *do* to her?" she whined. She couldn't help it. She wanted justice.

"Your sister and I will talk."

Katherine couldn't stand another minute. She rushed back to the stairs.

From the kitchen, her mother called, "Dinner in five minutes."

"I'm not hungry," shouted a disgruntled Katherine from halfway up the stairs.

"Good," said Rose from where she had followed Katherine out to lean against the base. "We've got company coming over and you eat like a cow."

Fists clenched, with one last parting shot Katherine yelled, "Well, at least I'm not a stupid whore."

Rose flipped her luscious curls over her shoulder as an evil smile crossed her glossy, ruby-red lips and she sauntered up the stairs. As she passed Katherine, she whispered in her ear, "At least I'm not a prude."

Katherine stared after Rose while a noxious mixture of envy, resentment, and anger filled her heart. That night she thought of all the things she would say to Rose the next day, all the comebacks, all the retorts she wanted to speak to her hateful older sister.

She never got the chance.

Rose was dead the next morning.

CHAPTER THREE

Getting up in the morning was always a struggle for Katherine. She hated mornings with a passion reserved for venereal diseases and warm soda. So when she emerged from the cocoon of her blankets, it was with the wariness of a cat expecting to get wet. She poked an arm out of her nest to check the temperature of the air in her bedroom first. When the chill of a too-cool room hit her flesh, she quickly snatched it back with an irritable grumble.

Curling in on herself with the cold flesh safely tucked back inside the warm blankets, she murmured, "I forgot to turn the heater on last night, didn't I?"

It was a regular occurrence with her, which meant that her room was now a freaking ice-box. She didn't bother poking her head out of the comforter to check the time displayed in red, glaring letters on her nightstand. She could sense the phases of the moon fine from under the covers. Dawn hadn't broken yet, and she knew from experience that the hardwood of her old floors would be cold; she had already felt the chill of the air and

 18

she knew a mad dash to the bathroom to turn the heater on was inevitable. But perhaps not for a few minutes more. With a satisfied smile she closed her eyes for more pleasant dreams. Dreams of her sister dropping into a whirlpool of mud, for instance. One that kept turning and turning and turning.

The next thing she knew, a knock rang loudly on her thick wooden door.

"Katy, Katy, wake up!" her mother commanded through the door.

Katherine heard her. She turned over and snuggled some more. She wasn't ready yet.

That wasn't good enough, apparently. With a jiggle of the doorknob, the Queen of Sandersville entered her daughter's room. Katherine heard her walk over to the bed in high heels through the blankets.

"Katherine Laine Thompson," her mother commanded. "Get up *right now*! It's only two hours until dawn, and you know how he gets if he doesn't eat all day."

"Just a few more minutes, Mom," said the bundle of covers.

"No, *now*! You have school in three hours and you need to take Gestap out for his breakfast."

"Why can't Rose do it?" said Katherine in faux-frustration. She knew the answer. Her mother came in her room every morning. The question-and-answer routine was always the same. It was almost comforting. Katherine knew what she was going to say before her mother even said it.

An irritable sigh echoed. "Because, as you know, Rose has the witches' council meeting every day before school…"

"As preparation for her rise to power," said Katy's irritated voice from beneath the blankets as she finished her mother's sentence.

"Yes," said her mother. "Now I'm off to take care of the shipping manifest for the shop. Do you need anything for your spells later this evening?"

"No," grumbled Katherine. "I've got everything but the lilac blossoms, and I'll get those when I take Gestap out."

"Good," said the queen as she turned and walked away, the echo of her high heels reverberating on the floor.

"Do you need me to pick up Rose from the council before I head to school?"

"No," said her mother. "She has her first out-of-town coven event later this morning. The guardian will be taking her and they'll be gone all day. I'll pack an explanatory note in your lunch for the human principal alongside the work she's already made up for you to give to her history and French teachers."

Katherine waited for the door to close. She didn't bother commenting.

"All right, Katherine?" said her mother in a leading tone.

"Yes, ma'am," said the blankets.

As the door closed, she said, "And Katherine?"

"Yes, Mother?"

"You know I appreciate your taking care of Gestap. Not everyone has the nature to handle him as you do, including your sister."

The door shut.

"You mean she's scared of him," grumbled Katherine as she hurriedly threw off the blankets and dashed for the bathroom.

Ten minutes later, she stepped out of a piping hot shower and threw on her sweater, jacket, and jeans. Stopping in the kitchen, Katherine grabbed an apple to happily munch on and made her way through the butler's pantry, the formal dining room, and out to the mud room off the back entrance. There she grabbed her mud-covered boots from the stack that she, her sister, and their mother kept for treks to the forest and when they went out riding. Although, to be honest, it was mostly her that did the trekking. They tended to rely on her to get the freshest ingredients for spells or ordered them online from the twenty-four-hour coven delivery service.

With a wry smile, Katherine grabbed her scarf off the door hook and remembered the first time her mother had told her about Broomstick Deliveries. She'd been so excited to see a *real* witch ride in on a broomstick like the storybook legends. Only to be quite disappointed to find out it was just clever marketing. The ingredients were acquired and stored by magic, but the delivery was anything but supernatural. In fact, it still surprised Katherine every single time she got an order of Himalayan mountain snow delivered by a woman with more metal in her face than on her Harley Davidson.

Broomstick Deliveries did an admirable job getting high-quality ingredients from hard-to-find locations, but to Katherine, there was still something special about walking through the moonlit forest to look for nocturnal salamanders or search ledge-by-ledge on the mountainside for glowing unicorn hairs trapped on branches. But the queen and her heir couldn't stand getting their outfits dirty, their hair snarled, or their manicures chipped. So she almost always went alone. Which was why Katherine had been surprised, to say the least, to be harangued into Rose's double-date only to find out it was outdoors. But leave it to the queen bee of Bethlehem High to venture into the middle of the woods and come out without a single hair in her French braid out of place.

Clearing her mind with a wry shake of her head, Katherine stuffed on the boots and walked out through the back gate to head toward the shed they kept in the backyard. As she approached it, her feet crunched down into the thin layer of snow that had accumulated overnight. It was barely a light frost and would disappear with the dawn of the sun in less than two hours.

As far as Katherine was concerned, that was a good thing. Rose romanticized the snow with all the merry feelings that it brought with it: the promise of hot cocoa in the parlor on All Saint's Eve and a bright fire burning over wooden logs in the fireplace. Katherine snorted just thinking about it. In the South, snow meant melting water in freezing cold temperatures, which usually meant black ice. A hazard on any road or trail, particularly when Katherine took her midnight steed, Black Fire, out on the forest trails for a gallop. It was ridiculous to think of snow as anything but a hazard at best, an inconvenience at worst.

As she approached the small shed, she took it in with a fond look. To an outsider it looked like a dilapidated and rickety shack made of tinfoil that sat forgotten and unattended in the backyard of the estate, close to an enclosed swamp and open to the elements with weeds springing up on either side. In reality, it *was* a dilapidated shed that was falling apart at the seams where its pre-fabricated metal walls leaned in to the interior with telltale signs of rusty red on their edges. And that was just the way Gestap liked it.

"Gestap, I'm coming in!" shouted Katherine as the moonlight shone down on the rusty old shed and the deceptively small swamp behind it.

With a grunt she grabbed hold of the metal door and pulled it back with a sharp yank of her elbow. It didn't make it easy—a loud protest of creaky metal emitted as the door swung back reluctantly and the edge caught in the dirt. Sighing, she stepped forward and into the darkness of the shed beyond. Grabbing a flashlight off of a nearby shelf from memory, she clicked it on. Or at least she tried to.

"Damn it, Gestap!" Katherine said in frustration. "Did the batteries die?"

No answer came forth from the darkness except the slight sound of water sloshing close by.

Katherine banged the long flashlight against her thigh. Hoping a jostle would get it going. It hurt her more than it did the flashlight, so she transferred the banging to the ground. Crouching down, she hit it in the soft packed dirt of the shed floor. She wasn't stupid enough to bang it against the shed wall. Gestap definitely would *not* like that.

With a flicker, the flashlight turned on. The beam of artificial light lit up the small interior of the shed and for the first time that morning, she saw the creature she got up before the crack of dawn every morning to tend to. Gestap sat in a pool of brown mud in the center of the shed, glaring at her. She knew he was glaring because the dark red orbs that served as his eyes were staring straight at her and he wasn't moving.

Katherine sighed, "I'm here, aren't I? Seriously, Gestap, what's your problem?"

He didn't move.

23

She glared at him. He glared back.

"Do you want breakfast or not?"

Slowly he rose from his seated position. As he rose, the mud sloughed off his head and down his slimy sides. Gestap looked like a giant toad with mottled green skin and purple dots everywhere. But no one would mistake his appearance for anything but deadly. He was the size of a Volkswagen Beetle and, more than that, he was a kobold. Every witch worth her salt knew what a kobold was. Every human that didn't want to be bled dry knew to stay away from him.

Ribbitt? He croaked from where he sat.

She stared at him in astonishment with her left hand fisted on her hip and the flashlight held tightly in the other.

"So you want to play games?" she said slowly.

Rib-b-itt?

Katherine groaned in disgust and turned away. "I'm going back to bed."

A masculine voice with the educated intonations of a British peer emerged from behind her retreating back. "Seriously, Katherine? I thought that was pretty funny."

She sniffed and turned to look over her shoulder. "You think *everything* is funny."

"Yep," said the toad-like kobold as he moved his front arms back and forth in the mud, letting noxious vapors drift up from where they'd settled under the still top layer.

"Eww, stop it," she snapped. "You know that stuff stinks to high heaven!"

"Stuff? This *stuff* is Indonesian hot spring mud imported directly from the islands mixed with pureed red snail intestines and black forest truffles." he said in a purr. "It's *perfect.*"

She turned around fully. "It stinks. Knock it off."

"Fine," he said while he sulked. "Leave it to you mortals to have no taste. Why, when I served the High Queen of Richmond, we bathed in the mixture *daily*."

She narrowed her eyes. "Really? I wouldn't put it past a sane woman to throw it out while you weren't looking."

"You jest, I'm sure," he said haughtily. "There is nothing like kobold mud baths to reduce wrinkling in the skin, and *boy*, did she ever need it. If you ever saw her naked, it was like a pig carcass hit with the black plague and then put in the drying machine with…"

"All right, enough!" said a horrified Katherine. "I really didn't need that image in my head. *Really* didn't want to know what the Queen of Virginia looked like, naked or clothed."

"Richmond!"

"What?"

"She's the High Queen of *Richmond*, Katherine," Gestap said. "You should know that. There are no high queens of the states, just the capital cities."

She glared at him. "Maybe I didn't. Maybe we're not all educated on the fineries of court. What's the difference? She might as well be the Queen of Virginia—nothing gets past any queen, high or not, in the domain she rules."

"Regardless, it's prudent in political circles to know who's who and where they rule. If you ever said that in court, you'd be laughed out," he said with a sniff.

"Whatever," said Katherine as she stomped to the back of the shed and undid the latch on the double doors that opened onto the swamp in the back.

"Not whatever."

"It's not like I'll ever have a chance to go to a high court. That's Mother's duty once a year, and then Rose's when she ascends to take her place."

Katherine reached over to grab the spear with the serrated blade on the tip from where it leaned against the inside of the shed. Turning her head to look over at Gestap, who had already hopped over, she walked out on the ramp with him by her side.

"One doesn't need to experience something to have knowledge of it," he tutted. If she wasn't so irritated with him, the sight of a massive toad tutting would have made her crack a smile.

As she took a seat in the small skiff tied next to his shed, she murmured, "Actually, I changed my mind. Rose isn't afraid of you. She's afraid of your mouth."

He didn't hear her, as he was busy happily diving into the swamp. As she waited for him to rise to the top of the moonlit waters, she pushed off from the ramp with help from the blunt end of her spear. Gestap soon emerged and took hold of the rope at the front of the skiff with his large mouth. With powerful kicks of his hind legs, they were off into the swamp.

She took in the waters around them, disturbed only by the ripples from his kicks. Huge lily pads and swamp cypress trees broke the surface frequently. The cypress trees in particular were magnificent to watch. Their massive trunks were so wide at the base that the trees looked like the round teepees of the Native American shamans who came to Georgia once a year to renew the sacred 1850 concord of Coven-Shaman Relations. The concord was one of many enacted by the witch queens in remembrance of the Trail of Tears beside their shaman brethren. Witches and shamans may not believe in the same gods and certainly didn't practice similar magic, but they did agree on the benefits of remembering the past and respecting their ancestors.

Katherine mused on the history of the original colonies as she sat back and the cool mist of the swamp enveloped her. As Gestap swam further in, he led the skiff on a convoluted path around and between the whispering trees. As Katherine tilted her head back to watch the fern-like foliage pass overhead, she relaxed, her body stilled, and the cool moistness of the earth, the distinctive smell of the flowering lilies, and the flicker of fireflies in the night surrounded her. When the lilac blossoms passed by, she made sure to grab a handful.

She listened to Gestap's swift but powerful strokes until they got to a platform in the center of the swamp. It was a recycled shipping crate that she'd brought out here years back after getting tired of stabbing prey from the unstable skiff. Stabbing the pole into the shallow waters that surrounded the platform, she vaulted off the skiff with the momentum it gave her with a grunt. And then she watched with wary eyes.

This time of the night was what the teens at her high school liked to call the witching hour. Little did they know they were right. It was the space and time just before the break of the sun's rays through night's passage. A lot of things could happen between now and dawn, and a lot of things did happen. She wasn't afraid. Just wary. She really didn't want to be late for homeroom. If there was anything she hated more than tardy attendance, it was having to slink into class in front of every single hot sophomore in Bethlehem High. The irony ran like a delicious thrill through her. A witch attending a human school named after a Christian sacred site. But you did what you had to do, and when you came from a family of matriarchs born to rule a small town, that included mingling with the locals. After all, Sandersville was eighty-percent human, following the trend of most witch/human population densities up and down the east coast.

Standing next to the edge, she watched Gestap circle around the platform with ease. She didn't urge him to hurry, because he wouldn't listen. While she waited for him to get his act together, her thoughts turned to what she was in for at school. For one thing, she wasn't the most popular kid. Being a small fish in an even smaller pond was what happened when fifty witches and warlocks attended a combined middle and high school of eight-hundred students.

Because she couldn't or wouldn't use her gifts unnecessarily, she was the target of every witch or wizard with a desire to climb the social ladder and the brains to realize she was vulnerable. Of course, her mother wouldn't step in.

I'd die of embarrassment if she did, anyway, Katherine thought to herself. What self-respecting teen had their *mom* take up for them?

She made light of it now, but her stomach flipped in unease. Being a queen's daughter had advantages…and one major disadvantage: anyone who wanted to hurt her mom could go through her daughters. Which was why they had guardians, and Katherine was sure that none of her tormenters had done much worse than putting exploding tomatoes in her locker. Rose had put a firm hand down as queen bee that no more stupid tricks were to be practiced on her sister at Bethlehem High without her say so after one particular incident had managed to make Rose collateral damage. Yet even that only made life more livable, but not necessarily comfortable.

Katherine shifted on the hard planks. It wasn't just her coven brethren that were a problem. She could deal with their childish antics well enough and she had a few friends...no matter what her sister said otherwise or her mother thought.

What bothered Katherine more than anything was that no matter what she said or how carefully she said it, the humans were afraid. She had to admit, they had reason to fear. They lived in a coven-controlled society, and they knew that no matter who they elected or what position they served, the witches and warlocks ruled the lands of their thirteen states. In fact, the superiority of coven members was the *only* thing the Coven High Council of the Thirteen Colonies seemed to agree on these days. Not only was the human government coven-controlled, but every queen ruled their territory with absolute authority. And not every queen chose to do so as fairly as her mother did. She had heard horrible tales of humans murdered over something as minor as a social slight farther south in Georgia. But everyone turned a blind eye to what happened outside of their own town or county. Over the years, she had a made a few attempts to make friends across human-coven boundaries. She'd even managed to have a sleepover with one girl. That had ended with an experience best left unexplained, except to say that the girl had left screaming with a live snake writhing in her hair. So for now, Katherine let her inter-species attempts at bonding go. She didn't have to like the way society was run, but she did have to live with it. The last witch to protest the injustice of coven rule in the countryside had been burned at the stake—by her own coven.

Fear tended to silence people, human and witch alike. In Sandersville, at least, the people were happy, the crops were fruitful, and the businesses run by human, coven, and others alike were protected by the queen's laws. Her mother didn't even require a queen's tax like her sister queens in most other areas. Which was why Katherine's family didn't have servants, she drove a ratty old Camaro, and Rose worked weekends at the local clothing boutique to buy the latest fashions out of New York.

That said, the money their mother did have went to making sure they had the best coven and human education possible. It put them in a strange position. Their mother was one of the few in Lancaster County that could both *afford* to have her daughters attend coven lessons and *wanted* her second daughter to have the opportunity. Most witches taught their first-born alone; after all, it was the first-born that was gifted with the most magic and the right to rule. Even if that just meant a farm on the edge of the county, the first-born witch would inherit her family's seat of power. It just so happened that Rose would inherit an entire town and the surrounding land.

Talking to Gestap absentmindedly, she said, "My birthday's in three weeks, you know."

Bubbles surfaced. She assumed he was speaking to her. She wasn't willing to stick her head in the water to find out, even though she was perfectly proficient in mer linguistics. And then it happened. The swamp water all around them began to bubble up as if she sat in the middle of a hot spring. Gripping the spear with the serrated tip held out in front of her, she waited anxiously.

CHAPTER FOUR

Before she could blink, Gestap leapt straight up out of the water with a swamp gator right on his tailless behind. The gator's white belly glistened as it emerged from the water and its maw was wide open to take a chunk out of the giant frog that rose above it. Then it all froze like a picture in a frame. The gator hung upright in mid-air while Gestap loomed above it with a smirk on his froggy face. It was almost comical to watch the gator immobilized by Gestap's magic—unable to move, unable to eat the succulent froggy meat just above him, and unable to save itself. Because now it was Katherine's turn. With a sharp push she thrust her blade into the under-flesh of its vulnerable belly and up into its heart for a clean kill.

Gestap landed on the platform next to her with a *wump*.

"Well done, Katherine," he said, pleased.

She turned to him with her hands on her hips. "You were supposed to get a *small* one. What's small about a six-foot gator?"

If a frog could shrug, he did. "The only male in the area."

Her eye twitched. "The only *gator* in the area?"

"Well, no," admitted the shifty kobold, "but you know how much I love to snack on the balls."

"Gestap!"

"Well, you asked."

"I did *not* ask you that," she said with a disgusted look. "We need to get back to the shed in thirty minutes, so get to it."

"Get to it?" said the mildly affronted car-sized frog.

She turned and glared into his large red eyes. There was no need to look down, since he was her height sitting on the platform.

With gritted teeth and a flourish of her hand, she said, "Oh, mighty kobold, would you commence eating your breakfast now?"

He sniffed. "All you had to do was ask."

She refrained from calling down a hail of lightning on his head like she wanted to.

Stepping back, she watched as Gestap hopped off the platform. In mid-leap he transformed into his true form. A creature half the size of a normal human with the appearance of a woodland sprite: two arms, two legs, homespun clothes, short-cropped hair and a generally mischievous expression. She actually preferred his toad disguise for two reasons: one, it didn't hide how dangerous he truly was; and two, Gestap tended to embrace his darker side more in his natural form. As a toad he was lazy. As she watched him climb up the gator's still form, she noted the subtle difference between a sprite and a kobold's form. The retractable claws appearing on his hands and the rows of razor-sharp teeth that she knew were in his mouth were dead giveaways to the kobold heritage. With a grunt, Gestap latched on to the pale under-flesh of the gator, tearing the belly to shreds and sticking his head completely into the cavity he had made.

Katherine turned away, disturbed. Even she couldn't watch this morning after morning. The only good thing was that she'd gotten so used to it that she no longer had to stop by the side of the road to puke up her guts on the way to school. She knew he was using the suckers in his tongue to drain the alligator dry of blood rather than eating the pure flesh, but he didn't have to bury his head in the creature to do that. He just liked to. With a shudder she realized he was also probably searching for the creature's reproductive organs with his long, prehensile tongue. Gestap didn't kid around about his breakfast.

It took him fifteen minutes of slurping, some chewing, and decidedly disturbing grunts before he was done. When he finished, the alligator dropped into the swamp waters with a splash. She heard the other gators who'd surfaced at the smell of the blood surround the corpse and feast on the entrails. She still didn't turn around. She'd made that mistake once before. The sight of Gestap's bloody serrated teeth and the vicious glee on his face had sent her ten-year-old self crying home to her mother in a swirl of dark magic. It had been the first and only time she'd ever teleported. Unfortunately, her aunt, the one who hunted demons in graveyards for fun, had been at the house and had frog-marched her back to the swamp to collect Gestap with a stern lecture.

Because as vicious as Gestap was, he was also loyal to her family. He was bound by blood to the witches of Sandersville after being kicked out of the courts up north for a reason he wouldn't disclose—and whatever it was it must have been *good* to be banished from seven different high-queen courts. According to the agreement he had with her mother, Gestap had to be led to and from his feeding grounds with the aid of a witch of the Thompson bloodline. Since Rose threw up at the very sight of blood, the queen couldn't be bothered to do it, Cecily was too gentle, and no one knew *where* Aunt Sarah was from day to day, that left Katherine to be his handler.

Soon she heard the sounds she associated with his transformation back into the form he preferred—the large and rotund toad. As she turned back and walked to the edge of the platform, he leapt into the swamp water to clean himself of entrails and blood. She hopped into the skiff without a word and they headed back to his shed. After taking *another* shower and hoping she didn't stink like gator guts, she headed into the garage with a prayer.

"Please gods, Mother of the Earth, Lord of the Skies, Tinkerbelle, *whoever* is out there," Katherine mumbled, "if you get me to school today, I will do everything in my power not to set anything on fire…or kill anyone. I pinky-swear, I'm on my best behavior."

As she opened the garage door, she looked at the car furthest from the door with disdain. Slowly Katherine walked by her mother's Lexus SUV, her sister's Volkswagen Beetle, and came to her own clunker, a 1982 Chevrolet Camaro that looked like it belonged on the set of that time-travelling 80s movie with the crazy professor. Staring at it glumly, she noticed that her three-year-old paint job was peeling—badly. She knew she shouldn't have taken it out to those two farm boys who swore up and down that they could do it up like an auto body shop. But she hadn't really had a choice. It was them or drive all the way to

Gainesville on fumes. Now she had a car with orange tiger stripes and chipping paint. It looked like a diseased stray cat.

Her main problem wasn't the paint job, though. It was the three-hundred-dollar malfunctioning carburetor, which had turned into a non-functioning starter, plus a messed-up thingamajig with a two-hundred-and-fifty-dollar price tag. She had already fixed the carburetor. She couldn't afford to fix the other two problems until she got the witches' brew she'd promised the town's only real mechanic—Cliff. He didn't trust medical doctors, which suited her just fine. If the man wanted to trade his three-hundred-dollar service for a brew that would cost him fifty dollars from a human doctor, that was okay by her.

For now, she just prayed. The starter worked…sometimes.

"All right, Marigold," she said nervously, "it's just you and me today."

Opening the driver's side door with a tentative pat of the hood, she slid into her comfortable seat lined with faux fur and palmed her jangle of keys to find the one to slide into the ignition slot.

As she turned her wrist a heartbeat later, Marigold coughed to life. Did she forget to mention that poor old Marigold had an oil leak, too? Katherine shut the driver's side door with a hard yank. If she didn't, the door tended not to close.

As Marigold warmed up, Katherine put a tired forehead down on the cracked leather steering wheel with a sigh. Once, just once, she wished the town had enough money to provide *both* of the queen's daughters with a car. She flicked the garage door button on her overhead visor and glared at Rose's brand-new Beetle with clenched teeth as the door behind her slowly rose.

She hated the style of the Beetle, but what she wouldn't give for a car that didn't leak oil like it was going out of style, didn't falter every mile, and actually *started* every time she wanted it to.

Swiftly she backed out of the garage and drove around the left side of the house's wraparound porch to pull out on the mile-long driveway. It was a straightforward shot to the road from there, so she stared at her home in the rearview mirror for a moment. The dawn had just begun to break, washing the white two-story home in a glow of red and orange. The burnt-red shutters stood out in the morning sun and the well-tended lawn showed off the prowess of her mother's natural command over the earth in her dominion. As she turned right at the gated entrance, Katherine had a wistful moment of desire to be back in bed, but she knew the faster she got to class, the quicker this day would be done. As she drove along, the windows shut as tightly as she could close them and the heater turned on full-blast, she hoped it would make it to the parking lot. Unfortunately, the heater conked out two miles down the road and banging on the dashboard did squat to make it work again.

"Oh well, can't have everything," she said to herself.

Eyeing the road, she thought of the nightmares she had about school. It wasn't really the people there that freaked her out. It was the people who *weren't* there that mesmerized her. In the middle of lectures, figures as whole as the freckled kid next to her would appear as ghosts made flesh. She could sense them like she could sense the coven members in her class. Mostly warlocks. But two witches had come, as well. They never spoke. At least not in voices that she could hear. But she knew one warlock's name.

Richard.

He was tall with dark hair, a dimple in his cheek, and always dressed stylishly. Like he was a model come to life from a fashion magazine. Whenever she saw him, her heart stopped. Unlike the others he only appeared for one reason—he was being tortured. Sometimes the clothes had yet to be ripped from his back, other times the invisible lash had already torn into his bare flesh. Every time he appeared, he disappeared with blood dripping down his side.

The only reason she knew his name was because he mouthed it. A lash would descend and his mouth would move—*Richard*. His bruised face would flinch as another blow landed—*Richard*. Sharp vertical cuts would appear on his stomach—*Richard*.

She supposed Richard could be someone else's name, but she knew in her heart that it was his. His through the pain, the misery, and the desperation reflected in his eyes. She knew he never saw her. But she would never forget him.

Nevertheless, she really didn't need him distracting her in homeroom. It was bad enough trying to manage her powers when she was upset; when she got frustrated on someone else's behalf, even a ghost's, it was impossible.

As she walked out of the parking lot, she gathered her courage. She knew today wouldn't be any worse than any other day, but that wasn't necessarily comforting. A cold sweat broke out on her brow as she shifted the strap of her book bag so that it hung off one shoulder. When she reached the front doors of the school, a cold chill took over her body. Startled, Katherine looked up. It was as if someone had stepped on her grave. The chill dissipated, but the air of foreboding around her didn't. She knew better than to try to shake it off—as a witch it was in her blood to read the signs into the forthcoming doom. But usually she had more to go on than a cold breeze.

The school bell rang out, disturbing her concentration.

"Hey, you going to open that door or what?" said a cautious voice behind her.

Turning around Katherine took in a guy with dreamy chestnut eyes, tightly-curled black hair, and a killer smile. Derrick's team captain and an honest person. Reluctantly she bit back her snarl as she realized that she was in fact standing in front of the only entrance on this side of the school with both steel handles gripped firmly in her hands. Swinging the doors open with an elaborate flourish, she said, "After you, Mark."

He grinned flirtatiously. "Ladies first."

Giving him an assessing look, Katherine turned back around and walked in front of the human. For someone who had no chance with her, he seemed like a good guy. Her homeroom class was just down the hall, close to her locker. She put the bag away and grabbed her binder and textbook for her first class of the day—math, a subject she enjoyed when she wasn't trying to figure out what a quadratic equation was.

Slipping into her seat in the very back row of homeroom, Katherine sighed in relief.

So far, so good.

The only blemish in her plans so far was the empty seat next to her. She wondered where Cecily was. It wasn't like her cousin to be late, even to a class as stupid as homeroom. Slipping out her phone, she quickly shot off a text in case Cecily overslept.

Five minutes later the bell had rung, all the stragglers had straggled into their seats, and no sign of Cecily had appeared on her phone or in class. Biting her lip, Katherine decided not to worry too much.

"She probably decided to skip this morning," whispered Connor from the row across from her. He was leaning back in his chair with his red hair flopped over in his eyes. She had known Connor since they were toddlers. He was confident, fluent in sarcasm, a pyro, gay, and possessed one of the coolest witch's gifts she'd ever seen: telepathy. She didn't even mind the telepathy part so much. It was the fact that he dropped in on her thoughts like they belonged to him that irritated her. But he was also the closest thing she had to a friend that looked human for miles…aside from Cecily.

She grimaced. "Maybe, but I doubt it."

"You worry too much, Katherine," he teased. "You're the second in line for the throne…"

"Which means squat," she hurried to protest. She hated when her friends brought it up. She wanted to distance herself as much as possible from Rose, which was hard enough when you went to the same school, lived in the same town, and there were less than two dozen witches and warlocks her own age for miles.

"Exactly," Connor said, eyes lighting up. "Don't you know that means party, party, party? Haven't you learned *anything* from the British royals?"

Katherine narrowed her eyes as a smirk appeared on his face and she threw a pencil at him. "Hush up, you."

A voice in front of the room, Mrs. Peabody, an English teacher and her homeroom advisor, said, "Is there something you wish to share with the rest of the class, Ms. Thompson and Mr. Lanchen?"

Katherine shrank back into her chair. "Umm, no, Mrs. Peabody."

"That's what I thought," said the white-haired woman with a sniff and a subtle push on her glasses.

"Now that I have you all for the next twenty minutes, why don't we discuss some literature?" Mrs. Peabody said eagerly.

A chorus of groans from the students in the class, human and coven alike, met her suggestion.

"Now, now," she said hurriedly, "I have something fun for you today. Who's heard of *Macbeth*?"

The room was silent.

"From Shakespeare," the old woman prodded, clearly not giving up.

Tentatively, a girl with long black hair pulled back in a butterfly clip raised her hand.

"Yes! Thu Kim?" Mrs. Peabody said, peering hopefully at the girl in the second row.

"He was a general who believed a prophecy made by witches in Scotland. It meant his downfall," said the girl, dropping her hand.

"The prophecy wasn't the cause of his fall," murmured Katherine disdainfully.

"Yes, and?"

Thu Kim shrugged. As she did so the clip in her hair fluttered and released. Her silken hair fell down around her face as the live butterfly fluttered above her head with spread wings trailing shimmering dust. Katherine wasn't sure if it was actual fairy dust or just glitter. Either way, it was cute. Holding up a finger for it to land on, Thu Kim transformed it back into a stiff hairclip with a hint of magic. Katherine smiled sadly, watching. She wished her witch's gift did simple things like that when it got out of hand.

"Miss Thompson?" said Mrs. Peabody.

Katherine flicked a startled gaze back to the front of the room. "Yes, Mrs. Peabody?"

"Shakespeare is a favorite of yours, isn't he?"

"Not especially," muttered Katherine.

"Oh?" said Mrs. Peabody. "I had hoped you would enlighten the class on the morals of a human general scheming with a pair of coven sisters based on the illuminating paper you wrote."

Katherine stared at Mrs. Peabody from the back of the room. So she was one of *those* people. Humans that did everything in their power to prove that witches and the people that served them were the spawn of Satan. A fable if she'd ever heard one. Not the demonic part, *those* were real, but everything else had been modified from true lore, shall we say.

She knew she shouldn't have written that diatribe against Shakespeare, obviously a favorite of Peabody's, for English class. But she hadn't thought the woman would call her on it in the middle of class.

Smiling sharply, Katherine spat out, "Well, then, I would say Shakespeare was a coward who deceived his patron queen, the great Elizabeth I, and betrayed the trust of the three witch sisters who entrusted him with their journals. He was never supposed to divulge the true histories of the coven council, and he paid for that."

"Much like a more modern author and the Sistine Chapel accords?"

Katherine replied simply, "Much like, Mrs. Peabody."

And then it happened. A ghost appeared. It wasn't Richard, thank the gods. It was one of the witches, the one Katherine had dubbed Anastasia after a local cat she knew with the same wavy chestnut hair. Anastasia looked upset, like she was shouting…no…arguing, with someone. She was raising her fist and shaking it while her mouth ran a mile a minute. Even though she was acting belligerent, Katherine saw fear in the ghostly woman's eyes. And then she startled as Anastasia fell to floor under a person's fists. A person she couldn't see. A fist she didn't know was there. But the bruises on Anastasia's face told her they were.

"Mrs. Thompson, am I boring you?" said Mrs. Peabody.

Katherine's vision snapped back into focus. But it was like being in two places at once. She couldn't help the girl who was falling to blows in the vision next to her or escape the diatribe of the irate teacher in front of her. Katherine stiffened. She wanted to do something, anything. But she knew it was no use. No one else saw the ghosts in her visions except her. When she tried to convince other coven members of what she saw, including her mother, they laughed her off. So she said nothing anymore. Not to anyone.

Silence descended over the classroom fraught with tension. Everyone waited to see what would happen next. Katherine *knew* what would happen. She would sit here quietly ignoring them both until this first period hell was over.

"No, ma'am," she said quietly as she deliberately avoided looking at the girl being beaten beside her by staring off into the distance. She couldn't help them, anyway. She never could.

CHAPTER FIVE

As Mrs. Peabody narrowed her eyes, sniffed, and then turned to pick on another student, Katherine drifted off. In a daydream, a memory, a premonition, or something that was all of those things in one. She watched through the frosty window as a maelstrom of black clouds, heavy lightning, and rain appeared in the morning sky.

For a moment she felt a sharp pain, the same kind she felt when her mother had fractured her knee surveying corn last week. She'd known the moment the Queen of Sandersville had fallen and had felt her mother's pain from miles away. She had asked Rose about it later. After chiding her about releasing a powerful flare of magic in response and setting an acre of forest on fire in the process, as if Katherine had had a *choice*, Rose had explained that she'd also started to sense the pain of others late in her fifteenth year.

But this ache was different. It was worse, and she had no idea what was causing it. Then she felt her gifts rise. The dark gifts. The dangerous part of her that was her witch's gift. The part of every witch and warlock's magic that was innate to them, unique to them. That one special gift that made every coven member different from the rest. That couldn't be duplicated with spells or trapped with magic. Rose's was her affinity to plants. Their mother's was her command over earth. But Katherine's was unlike either of those. It wasn't weird and unique, like Thu Kim's ability to awaken awareness in inanimate objects, or cool, like Connor's telepathy. No, hers was a call. A call that brought destruction in its wake.

With a shock, Katherine snapped out of her vision. She could feel her power building in a swirl of darkness in the pit of her stomach. Like a twister, it was ready to emerge. Standing up in a hurry, she ran between the desks in an effort to get out the door. To get somewhere quiet. Somewhere safe where she wouldn't hurt anybody.

She was holding on by a thread.

A thread that broke when Mrs. Peabody snapped, "Katherine Thompson, *sit down!*"

The magic surged up through her like a geyser erupting. She fell to the floor, trying to contain it, and was barely aware when Connor came up behind her hunched-over form on the cold floor.

"Easy, Katherine, take it easy," said Connor as he put a hand on her back.

His touch was a comfort. People might gossip about his prying ways, but he had her back when she needed it. But it wasn't enough. Fortunately, there were other witches in the room who knew what was coming. She might have been a social pariah, but they recognized a building of magic when they felt it.

Standing up, Thu Kim whirled around and shouted, "Everybody down!"

The humans didn't hesitate. Jocks, nerds, and band geeks hit the floor like a bomb was going off.

With moments left, Thu Kim used her decorative butterfly to cast a protective spell over all the humans. It grew to inhuman proportions and spread its glowing wings over the cowering humans like a benevolent god.

Mrs. Peabody, who was stupid enough to still be standing, chose that moment to squawk, "What is going on?"

Thu Kim turned a laser-like glare at her. Without hesitating, she pulled off the rope of jade beads around her neck and tossed them at Mrs. Peabody. The necklace elongated until it was more than three feet long and then it wrapped around the shocked human teacher like a boa constrictor. The teacher collapsed to the floor bound, gagging, and screaming through the beads in her mouth.

Then the mists came like wraiths on the wind. Darkness claimed the sun and the screams started. Outside the classroom and within. Katherine's power wasn't a gift that called on nature, like Rose's gift. It wasn't the green forest that responded to her call. No, she called death. And death responded to her like a hound heeling to his huntsman.

Katherine turned her horrified gaze to the windows, expecting Death to come forward as a man riding on the stormy front to exact his price. But even she could not have foretold what appeared.

At the moment, death was not one entity, but many. Death came as hunters riding on a maelstrom of lightning and thunder like the fabled Seelie hunt of olden times. Standing on shaky legs, Katherine looked into the dark clouds rolling through the sky with ominous potency. She could see five ghostly riders. Five harbingers of death.

She knew they were *her* riders. Instinct told her that they were hers to command. But on the three separate occasions when they had appeared in the past fifteen years, only once had they heeded her words. Their will was their own.

She turned to Connor with dread in her eyes as the gale-force winds from the maelstrom shattered the windows along the wall.

"When one was called last week, an acre of forest burned in penance. Plants, animals, and fey died," she said haltingly. "With five called, more must die."

Connor looked at her, his face blanched of any color. He had never seen her witch's gift in practice. Many whispered about it, but until they saw it in action even they didn't believe it was possible to call beings from the Other world.

"How do they choose?"

She swallowed. "They don't deliberate, if that's what you're asking. But they've always struck down the source of my ire swiftly."

"And today that is?" he said his voice dipping into hysterics.

"I don't know," she said. "I haven't a clue. *I* didn't call them. They responded to something else."

"You're sure?"

She shrugged. "I saw the ghosts today. But they're not here. I felt pain but don't know the source. I don't know why they're here." Her voice was starting to slide into the deep end of the panic scale.

"Then why can't you just call them off? Tell them it was a mistake. You need a murder-for-hire rain check. *Whatever*."

"Because they never listen to my pleas," she said harshly. "I reach out to them accidently and they respond. They wreak their vengeance. They leave. That's the existent of our relationship."

"Fuck me. Seriously, what kind of witch are you?" said Thu Kim while looking over at them. Her voice was half-horrified, half-derisive.

Connor turned to Katherine and put both hands on her shoulders. "Listen, sweetie. That *might* have been the extent of your relationship before, but now, more than ever, you need to get to first base. No ands, no ifs, no buts about it. Now get out there and talk to them."

He let go and gave her a push toward the window.

Katherine didn't turn back. He was right. She couldn't keep ignoring them like the ghosts that kept appearing around her. These beings affected her whenever they appeared, and it was high time that she got a handle on *why*.

She walked forward, past the desks strewn haphazardly, past the huddled mass of students on the floor, past Thu Kim, who stood defiantly next them. She gave her a nod. The girl, she'd never spoken to, gave a nod back and said, "Kick their asses."

Nothing else needed to be said.

Katherine stepped over broken glass on the window ledge out into the yard beyond. Distantly she heard the sirens of the school go off in warning. Better late than never.

Now all of the classrooms would be locked down. No one would come after her.

The fierce winds outside whipped her dark hair back and forth as she walked forward in determination to face down her nightmares.

The five riders came down on horseback from the clouds like avenging gods returning to Earth. As they met the ground, the mists and lightning around them dissipated. It was just her and them. Oddly quiet. Oddly serene. They said nothing. They were all different, shifting in and out of her vision with changing appearances so that she couldn't quite grasp which was which.

"Why are you here?" she asked.

They didn't answer. Just stared down at her from horseback.

"What do you want?" she tried again. Still no response.

Frustrated, tired, and afraid, she decided there was nothing else that her magic could throw at her, so she poured her gift out and into the harbingers of death before her.

The *least* they could do would be to answer her query.

The middle one pushed its horse forward. "We come at your bidding, High One."

Surprise rocketed through her. It had worked.

And then death smiled. "No, but we will answer your query."

Her surprise promptly sank into irritation.

"Why are you here?" she repeated.

It looked off in the distance. "Because death comes for you."

"You *are* death," she pointed out.

"No, that is what you call me in your mind's eye. We are your Riders, your Protectors, your Guard."

Her jaw dropped. "My guard from *what?*"

"Your enemies."

"I don't *have* any enemies."

 48

It turned its distant gaze back to her. "They will come. They already have taken two of your family. They will take more."

Then it turned its horse around and the others followed suit.

"Wait, what do you mean *they*?" she asked desperately.

"You must go," he said.

"Go? Go where?"

"To the dark queen's court."

There was only *one* dark queen that she knew of, and she ruled the city of Atlanta—her great aunt. The same great aunt's whose court was off limits, courtesy of her father's deathbed proclamation. She spluttered, "Uh, no can do."

He didn't turn around or contradict her.

"When your blood flows on the starlit floors, you will call on us. And we will come."

Before she could say another word, they disappeared in darkness and mist. The sky cleared. Glass crinkled behind her.

She turned to see everyone in her class standing at the window, staring in fear and astonishment.

She swallowed. Looked at Connor. The same emotions showed on his face.

More reasons to fear the most broken witch in Bethlehem High.

Swallowing, she turned and left. Going to the parking lot. Going to Marigold. There was one person who she could talk to this about. One person who understood. She had to find Cecily.

Behind her she heard Connor say, "Katherine, wait!"

But he didn't come after her. Even he wasn't that stupid.

As she turned the corner, Katherine was shocked to see three SUVs peel into the school parking lot at top speed. Out of the cars poured guardians in three-piece suits and her mother just behind them. She blinked while thinking aloud, "That was fast." Her mother was hyperaware of her powers and grew quite upset whenever she 'used' them, but even for her this was unreal.

One of her mother's guards swept into the school while another came up to her with a brisk, "Keys, please."

"What?" Katherine said while looking at him in a daze. She was starting to get scared. The queen was moving stiffly and the guards surrounding her were armed with enough magical protections to take out a S.W.A.T. team.

"To your car," he explained in a clipped voice.

She handed over the jangle of keys with a muted point to the mangled mess that was Marigold in the parking lot. Walking past him, she ducked between guards to get to her mother.

"Mother, I'm sorry. I didn't mean..." Katherine started to say. Then she got a close-up look at the queen's face. As her mother took off her sunglasses, Katherine could see that her eyes appeared bloodshot, her makeup was ruined, and her hair was in disarray. Now, *that* was scary. Her mother never looked anything less than immaculate. Unlike Katherine, who'd once shown up to class with rollers still in her hair because she had forgotten to check the very top layer.

"Mother, what's wrong?" she whispered.

Her face crumbling, the Queen of Sandersville took her youngest daughter's hands in her own and gripped them tightly. "Something has happened to your sister, Rose."

Katherine sucked in a gasp as she looked around as if expecting Rose to appear like magic.

"What? What happened? Did she get hurt? Is she in the hospital? How?"

Katherine knew that despite the availability of coven healers, her mother had always preferred to take her daughters to human doctors first, witch healers second. She said it was more sanitary. Rose thought she was hiding something, but what even she hadn't been able to guess.

Katherine watched as her aunt emerged from the SUV behind them with a characteristic glare pasted on her face. The queen shook her blonde hair as her lips trembled and she practically collapsed in her Dolce & Gabbana pumps. "She's dead. Our Rose is dead."

Then Katherine's world really dropped out from under her.

CHAPTER SIX

As she watched the raindrops roll down the dark-tinted windows of the SUV her mother, her aunt Sarah, and she rode in, questions like *how* and *when* rolled through her mind. Turning to the queen, who sobbed quietly into her sister's shoulder, Katherine had to wonder *why*.

Why had Rose died today? So soon, too soon. Katherine had thought she had a lifetime of arguments with her sister left. She never imagined she would wake up the next morning and find her gone...forever.

Sitting up stiffly, her mother blew her nose into a handkerchief. "Katherine, when I saw you at the school, I felt it—I felt your magic. You *used* your witches' gift."

Her tone was accusatory. Her voice hinted at betrayal even amidst her sorrow.

Katherine turned to her and swallowed deeply. "It was an *emergency.*"

Her aunt's eyes narrowed. "Your life was in danger?"

"No," protested Katherine. "It was more of a response to everything else happening around me. Our English teacher is horrid. I felt Rose's death—I'm sure that's what caused my gifts to surge this time, and on top of that the ghosts kept coming…"

"I told you not to talk about them!" shouted her mother.

Katherine narrowed her eyes. *Of all of the things for her to focus on, why them?* She wondered.

Even if it was out of character for her, it was ridiculous for her mother to keep pushing the topic of their appearance aside. They were *real*, Katherine was sure of that. With each passing incident it was also clear as daylight that the trigger of her powers could be connected to them.

Katherine sighed and rubbed her brow. *I haven't even told her about the riders yet*. Looking at her frazzled mother, she wasn't sure now was the best time to bring them up, either. It would be better to push the ghosts than try and convince her she now had other realm protectors. Wryly, Katherine thought to herself, *only to a witch would ghosts be more normal than fae*.

"But Mother, I feel like they're real, like I *know* them."

The queen's face trembled and her hands fluttered at her sides as if she wasn't quite sure what to do with them. But her voice was steady, even angry, when she said, "Katherine, weren't you listening to me? Your sister has *died*. Leave the ghosts alone."

But that steady anger didn't last for long. As if the very mention of Rose's unfortunate end brought back unwanted memories, the queen collapsed into her sister's arms again.

Katherine turned away from her glaring aunt's glowing red eyes and looked out the window again. So this was how it was going to be then.

She thought about what her mother had said when they first arrived in the car, before the hysterics had started. Before the never-ending waterworks had come. Her explanation of Rose's death had involved a downed airplane, Rose's boyfriend Derrick on life support, a vanished guardian, and a dead heir to the Sandersville throne. Even if the plane that Rose had been on had malfunctioned, Katherine knew that the guardian could have saved Rose by teleporting her to safety. Hell, that was his one and *only* job. So why hadn't he? Whatever the reason, this could not have been an accident. A witch, a warlock, and a guardian didn't die by plane crash. It just didn't happen.

As she watched the road to their house come into view, Katherine had one question on her mind.

Why had someone killed Rose?

They arrived home and the guards deployed in a ring outside. Katherine trembled from magical exhaustion and shock as she walked through the front door. Shock that the sister she hated would never be there to tease her again, never be there to smirk at her as she sauntered through the house, never be there to chide her for doing something wrong. Every incident she could think of that involved Rose came with a bad memory. But dammit, Rose had been *her* bad memory, her evil sister, her pain in the neck, and now that was gone.

As her mother stumbled up the stairs in tears—presumably to go to her room—Katherine hurried to latch on to her aunt's arm.

"Are they sure?" Her voice trembled.

Aunt Sarah turned to her. "They identified the remains magically and forensically. She's dead."

Katherine nodded her head in regret. Refusing to let the tears fall.

 54

"A demon?"

"If it was, it was traveling at four hundred miles per hour."

Katherine looked at her with incomprehension. "Is that possible?"

Her aunt barely kept herself from rolling her eyes with impatience. "No demon in existence could catch up to a Learjet."

Katherine racked her brain for something she could come up with, *any* explanation. Frustrated, she asked, "What about *Derrick?*"

Her aunt raised her eyebrows. She didn't say, 'Who?' but Katherine got the feeling she didn't know who Derrick was, and, more importantly, from the derisive expression on her face, she couldn't care less.

"Rose's boyfriend," Katherine hurried to explain. "He was a wind warlock... Surely he would have done something or known what happened...what attacked them."

Thinning her mouth into a thin line, Aunt Sarah said, "We still don't know if it *was* an attack...but if you must know, the other male on the vessel lived. We'll question him when or if he arises from his deathbed."

With that, she yanked her arm away and turned to hurry up the stairs after her distraught sister.

Leaning back again the front door with a *thump*, Katherine whispered, "What was Rose doing in an executive jet? And where was she going?"

Racking her brain, she remembered her half-awake conversation with her mother from this morning. Rose was supposed to be going away on coven business 'out of town,' but as far as Katherine knew, coven business was always the next town over. Never across county lines, much less the state.

"Cecily would know," Katherine said as she looked upstairs with a gleam in her eye. With her divination skills and something from Rose's room, maybe Cecily could even find out what happened to her sister. Good thing Katherine knew just where Cecily was. If her cousin had skipped school, there was only one other place she would be—the shop.

Rushing up the steps two at a time, she grabbed one of Rose's favorite scarves from her room and stuck her head in her mother's door. "Mom, I'm going to see Cecily at the shop!"

The queen turned devastated eyes to her only living daughter. "For how long? We-we have to make plans." Sobs interrupted her sentence.

Katherine wrinkled her nose. She had always hated displays of emotion, especially ones with large amounts of tears. In her opinion, crying wouldn't help Rose, action would.

"Not long. She'll need help closing up the shop early if you're not there anyway."

The queen thought about it as she gripped her sister's gloved hand tightly. "You're right."

"Aunt Sarah, is there anything you want from the shop or for me to tell Cecily?" Katherine said, peering over at the woman who was Cecily's mother and wore enough kohl eyeliner to be a pharaoh of the Nile Empire.

Aunt Sarah sniffed in disdain. "Nothing except that I'll be away for the next few days—to retrieve Rose's remains."

"Right," said Katherine, slowly backing away.

As she closed the door, she said, "I'll tell Cecily she's staying here, then."

"No, you will not," said her aunt sharply.

Katherine blinked at her around the half-closed door. "Why the hell not?"

"Katy, manners!" snapped her mother through tears.

Katherine grimaced. "Why ever not, dear Aunt Sarah?"

Glaring at Katherine as if she was stupid, her aunt said, "Because I need her to watch *our* house."

Katherine opened and closed her mouth. She wanted to say their house would be fine. Those damn carnivorous plants would live and the fire-breathing goat would certainly survive. She wanted to say that she *needed* Cecily as much as her mother needed her sister. But she didn't.

"Katherine, dear," said her mother quickly before her fiery daughter could say something she would regret.

"Yes, Mom?"

"I think I need you to see to some things around the town for the next two days while I deal with this. You and Cecily can do it together. You're old enough. After that you can check on Sarah's house. How does that sound?"

Katherine gritted her teeth. "It sounds great, Mother."

They both turned to look hopefully at her demon-hunting aunt, who shrugged. "It suits me."

"Great," muttered Katherine as she slipped out and closed the door.

Through the door she heard her mother scream, "Take two of the guardians with you!"

Katherine decided that she *didn't* hear that part.

Standing at the front door, Katherine pushed back the window curtains that hung to either side to assess the situation.

She could only see a few guards. So she dipped into her powers, second nature by now, to check their auras. She could sense six guards ringed around the house like a horseshoe. The two closest to the shed were already dealing with Gestap's irate demands—she could tell that from their angry red auras. The others that made up the guards coming up on the left and right side of the property had more sedate orange auras.

To her surprise, no guards were directly in front of the house. Narrowing her focus, she felt two auras farther out near the front gates.

"Must be the missing two guards," she murmured to herself. With a smile she noted that they'd parked their big black SUVs in a row on the front lawn.

"Don't mind if I do," she said while slipping out the front door quietly.

There was no way she could get Marigold off the property quietly, much less without the threat of breaking down. Marigold was a delicate creature. These SUVs were monsters ready to be let loose. Opening the driver's side of the one closest to her, she slid into the seat and hunched over. Quietly shutting the door, she got to work pulling large hairpins from her hair. She always kept them on hand for situations like this.

"Well," she admitted with her mouth full of hairpins, "not *exactly* like this."

Marigold tended to breakdown or malfunction twice a week like clockwork. Katherine had gotten *very* good at patchwork fixes. Plus she lost her keys like the dickens and sometimes needed a fast way to start the engine—that is, when the starter had actually worked. With a little magic, the hairpin as a conductor, and a lot of luck, she got the black SUV to start.

Smiling, she sat up fast—only to see the guards running around the house with guns drawn.

Eyes wide, Katherine put the truck in reverse and gunned the gas. The SUV shot backwards toward the tree line like a bat out of hell. She quickly corrected her course with a swerve of the wheel while praying the guards didn't start firing at her.

She heard them shouting as they ran forward. Her name came up. They recognized her. *Good.* They wouldn't shoot her, then. Putting the SUV in drive, she set off down the driveway at sixty miles an hour. Breezing past the gate and the guards who quickly dove out of the way, she hit the pavement with a squeal of tires.

She had the absurd feeling that Rose would be pleased. Hell, she was getting out of the house and doing it in *style*.

Making her way from the house to the shop from there was easy. She actually felt a hint of disappointment that the guards hadn't tried to follow her. It had felt daring, exciting, and a bit like being in one of those cop shows when she pulled out of the front yard. But she dreaded hearing what her mother would say when she got back.

As she parked in front of the store, she said to herself, "Let's put off going home as long as possible. I'm more likely to survive that way."

Stepping out of the black behemoth with a fond pat on the SUV's hood, Katherine pocketed the keys and walked up to her family's shop. Run by the Thompson line of queens since before her great-grandmother wrested control of the town and all of its inhabitants from her Cajun partner, to Katherine it was a second home. She had been toddling across its ancient and knotted hardwood floors since she was three, so she knew the northwest corner had a moldy-growth of spores that the sprites loved to take a nibble out of. Katherine also knew that her mother used those same spores for her tempest teas. But that wasn't even in the top one-hundred greatest things about the shop. In her top ten memories of the shop would be the time she had seen an archangel descend from the rafters, and all the times she'd crafted more spells than she could count on the ancient wooden table in the shop's center that held the register and assorted packages in progress.

Now she sighed in relief as she noted the "We're Open" sign on the front of the shop door. Cecily must be holding down the storefront. Only family ran the shop, and Katherine could count the members of her family in Sandersville on one hand, all female, too—Mother, her aunt, Cecily, herself…and Rose. A sharp-edged smile of sorrow and resentment crossed Katherine's face as she thought of her sister. The sister that she had just been arguing with at the foot of the stairs last night. The sister who had been alive until fateful events this morning.

"I guess I don't need all five fingers anymore. Not to count family, anyway," Katherine said sadly. She walked into Thompson's Apothecary and Herb Shop with the jangle of doorbells above her ringing away.

As soon as she entered into the store that smelled like herbs and ground cinnamon, she stopped cold and groaned aloud.

If the day could possibly get any worse after destroying her classroom it just did. Being told she had to go see her evil great aunt, finding out her sister was dead and peeling out of her yard with a guaranteed grounding for a month when she got back, had nothing on this new encounter.

The one person in town she dreaded seeing more than the demon-hunting aunt she'd left behind at the house stood in the middle of the herbal shop staring at her.

Ethan Warner leaned back against a wooden table covered in herbs, glass jars, distillers, and tools. His expression was unreadable. To everyone but her that is. Frustration lined his face.

Well, he could take a number.

Closing the door behind her, Katherine glared at him. As she stalked forward she stared at his well filled-out frame. He hadn't changed a bit. Still drool worthy. Still untouchable. He stood at least six-feet-tall with a firm body visible under his blue cotton T-shirt. Washed out jeans, Timberland boots, and crossed arms completed his disgruntled appearance.

Swallowing, she walked forward to greet the boyfriend she hadn't seen, heard from, or talked to in over six months.

"Katherine," Ethan said coolly as he rose from his slouched position.

"Ethan," she practically snarled back. "What can I do for you?"

Her exterior was furious. Her interior was ready to break down and cry. She hadn't seen Ethan in six months for a very good reason. They had broken up for a very good reason. Her sister had called her a prude for a very good reason. And it was a reason that she did *not* want to face right now. Not when it felt like the world was ending and she was going right along with it down the bath drain.

"Rough day?" he said, amusement crossing his face as he took in her disturbed appearance. She wasn't sure if it was her wind-tossed hair, rumpled appearance, or mascara-streaked face that was the most amusing, but it didn't matter anyway.

A tic developed in her eye. She reached up to the snarled mess of hair on top of her head before dropping her hand with a red blush on her face.

"Rough day?" she said softly. "Yeah, you could say that."

His demeanor didn't change as he looked her up and down like a pig before auction. Dryly, he said, "Even for you, this is a bit much. You know…looking like a night hag isn't going help you win over that football player."

For once Katherine was mystified. "What?"

Ethan's face darkened as if she were deliberately playing with him. "The guy you went to go see yesterday."

Katherine looked him in disbelief. "Don't tell me you're *jealous*?"

"Of Kevin?" Ethan said as he paced forward aggressively. "Not a chance. Just thought you had better taste than dumb jocks."

"And I thought you had better things to do with your life than stalk me?"

Anger flashed through his eyes. "I wasn't *stalking* you, the whole town was talking about you showing up at a bar looking like you tumbled through a bed of weeds."

"Tumbled is right," muttered Katherine distastefully. "And people need to mind their own goddamned business."

"What about me?" he taunted. "Should *I*?"

"Yes, because who I'm with is none of your goddamned concern! You made that clear six months ago."

Ethan cursed. "Well, I'm sorry, Your Highness, for still caring about you shacking up with a loser."

Katherine was visibly shaking with anger. She was so upset that she crossed her arms and grabbed each elbow to keep lightning from shooting from her hands. One of the perks of her witches' gift was the high probability for deadly and destructive accidental magic.

Ethan saw her move her hands to stop the flow of magic from releasing.

He asked, "What in the world is *wrong* with you? Even you have better control than this."

Katherine felt her anger tip into rage. If there was one time she wished her *protectors* that appeared with no warning and no call, would just appear in a maelstrom and descend in a homicidal rage, it was now. But they didn't really respond to her calls, as so aptly expressed by their leader. They did what they wanted to do.

"Yeah, well, my sister died. Or didn't the gossipmongers in town tell you that?"

Ethan's expression dropped into sorrow. "Katherine, I didn't know. I'm sorry, I…"

"I don't care about your 'sorrys' right now. Just get *out*! Because, as you pointed out, my control is kind of out the window, you being a bastard isn't helping, and so help me God, if I see you still in this shop within the next minute, I will unleash a bolt of lightning so powerful you'll be fried to a crisp," she snapped.

His expression immediately changed. His hands dropped to his side as he said, "Katherine, I'm sorry. I didn't know."

"Get out," she said tightly.

He looked at her with pity in his eyes. She looked at him with rage in hers.

Without another word, he exited the shop.

Katherine slowly lowered her arms, trying to rub the magical friction out of each arm as she did, and let out a deep sigh. She refused to cry. Today wasn't a day for tears. Her sister wasn't even home yet, let alone buried with all the sacred rights of a future queen. No, she would cry when it was over. Not before.

Now…now she had to find Cecily.

CHAPTER SEVEN

Not being able to stand a minute more alone with her thoughts of Rose and Ethan, Katherine rushed through the storage and down the three shorts steps into the storage room. It went a lot deeper in the ground than that, with a cellar on the bottom level for the things best kept in darkness and surrounded by the chill of the earth, but this initial basement was normal. With normal products—a normal mop and broom, wooden shelves made by human hands, and a spotless interior. As she caught her breath and fought not to hyperventilate from the anger coursing through her, Katherine looked around. Being around Ethan in general tended to make her upset. Being around him today of all days, when her sister was dead and her school looked like a tornado had run through it…courtesy of her anger…infuriated her. She wouldn't allow thoughts of why that was so to course through her brain. Rehashing her past with him was the *last* thing she needed on her mind today.

Taking a deep breath and muttering to herself to stay calm...
She wouldn't want her protectors to show up for the second time
in a row on the same day after all.

"That *would* be a record," she whispered to herself while
shutting her eyes and clenching her fists to force the ill thoughts
away. Then a dark realization came upon her. One of
shock...and trepidation.

The protectors haven't killed anyone today, Katherine realized.
She ignored how serial-killerish that sounded for the moment
and shuddered. There had never been a time those protectors
had appeared and they *hadn't* killed someone.

How is that possible? Katherine wondered to herself.

Control, whispered a voice inside her.

Then another voice spoke, but this time it was aloud. It was
Cecily.

"Control," she heard but didn't see Cecily muse aloud. "I
need the *control* for the verbena, otherwise this spell wouldn't
work."

Katherine shook her head hastily but kept her eyes shut and
slumped her shoulders. She wasn't a fool, but she had hope. Just
a minute more and maybe *one* good thing would come from this
day. She had thought...just for a moment...that she had her
own personal spirit guide.

Spirit guide...ancestral guardian...token mascot, she thought to
herself. *I'll take anything right now.*

Some witches were blessed with them. Ancestors whose spirits
reanimated to guide them through their witching hour. The
witching hour was the time between darkness and the break of
dawn as well as the time in a witch's life when she or he not only
assumed their greatest strengths but all their inherited

weaknesses. Between the ages of sixteen and twenty their gifts grew, their blood resounded with like witches, and their fates became aligned with their natural path. As much as Katherine had made fun of the Labrador, he and her sister had found each other, their blood had run afire when they were together—or so Rose had said—and his magic complemented hers.

"Derrick," she whispered to herself harshly as she leaned back on the door that wasn't far off, considering how short the steps were, both in width and height. Katherine may not have respected her sister and her sister's choice of a mate in life, but she certainly would in death.

"Although it couldn't have been that hard to find him," she said. "They went to the same schools all their life and were nominated and *won* prom titles in their sophomore year."

Meanwhile she was hiding out in dark forests with a kobold her sophomore year.

She opened her eyes with a sigh to really *see* the cellar. As her eyes slowly adjusted to the dimness of the cellar, she let the hope inside her die as she acknowledged that no more whispers were coming. She had walked into the room in a storm of anger from memory. Going up and down those same three steps from kindergarten until now had its advantages. Her mind had interjected all the familiar sights and sounds of walking down into the room, but just as her fists were clenched by her side in a physical attempt to ward off unwelcome thoughts, her eyelids were shut tight to banish the visions of Ethan hovering in her gaze. She almost laughed. It was such a childish response. To close your eyes and hide under the covers until the monster was gone.

"Well, at least I faced this monster head-on first," she whispered wryly to herself as she slowly unclenched her fingers and winced when she felt her nails ease from her flesh, assuredly leaving reddened half-moon marks behind. Then she opened her eyes and looked around. Her eyes took in the semi-dark room with rectangular windows high up on the wall, like peepholes only larger.

Katherine grumbled to herself in a distracted tone as she looked around with the light from the windows filtering down to form pools of sunlight encased by thin slivers of darkness where the pools didn't overlap. When she spotted Cecily, it was as if the cloud of anger around her dissipated like smoke, instead leaving a knot of anxiety in her breast. Here was someone who she could talk to. Someone who understood her better than anyone else in their small town: Cecily Carmichael.

Katherine stared up at her cousin with a slight smile on her face. Cecily's hair was pulled up into a messy ponytail with brown spiral ringlets bouncing every which way like a living thing on the back of her head and more tame curls framing her face that Katherine couldn't see but knew were surely arranged in an attractive manner. Her hair always was. Where Rose was…had been…drop-dead gorgeous with her perfectly coiffed hair, layered makeup, and expensive taste in clothes, Cecily was pretty in an effortless way. Her radiant smile could brighten a dull spring day; her eyes were framed by charming round spectacles which always seemed to be dipping towards the edge of her nose, and the dusting of freckles across a slightly brown face pointed to a mixed-heritage background. Katherine wasn't sure of Cecily's father background, she wasn't even sure *what* he was. She and Cecily had speculated on it endlessly as children, but aside from one fiery incident with Aunt Sarah, they had quickly realized that it wasn't a subject to bring up with the older members of their family, including long-distance relatives who probably didn't know anyway.

The only thing Aunt Sarah would say was that he was from a faraway land and the simultaneous best and worst thing that had happened in her life. Katherine was firm in her belief that he was someone wildly beautiful from a land like Morocco, but Cecily loved to point out that her mother hadn't traveled to North Africa, only East Africa and India, so he had to be something like Ethiopian or Nepali. Wherever he had come from, his daughter had been born with a natural beauty and vivacity. Cecily could light up a room whenever she walked in…any room that didn't contain her mother, that is. Cecily had inherited the light brunette color of her bouncing curls from her mother, darker skin from her father that Katherine envied in the summer for its radiance, and a brilliant personality all her own that sparkled through her hazel eyes.

As Katherine stood at the foot of the steps, her hands awkwardly twisting behind her, she waited for Cecily to acknowledge her. For Cecily to turn around, take one look at her, and realize that something was wrong.

But Cecily's mind was wholly concentrated on her task. Katherine gave a small smile. That was just like her cousin. Once her mind focused on something it was hard to distract her. Katherine wasn't sure if Cecily had guessed that Ethan had walked through the storeroom door and was going to silently wait on her. Or if she just hadn't heard the door open at all, but either way it was Katherine who would have to initiate contact.

Walking over to her brunette cousin, she watched as Cecily reached high above for a mason jar full of fresh herbs while standing on a ladder.

"Need some help?" asked Katherine, her voice odd as she braced the ladder.

"Oh, thanks!" said Cecily quickly as she descended down the ladder steps holding the medium-sized jar.

When she got to the last step and turned, Cecily paused her outstretched hand. She had gotten one good look at Katherine's face and frowned. "What's wrong?"

Katherine had been expecting her to start crying, since Cecily was emotional where Katherine was usually stoic. But…well…it hadn't occurred to her that no one had informed her cousin of a death in the family. There were only so many people to call to notify in case of an emergency like this and her mother was usually meticulous about such matters. But then again, neither of her daughters had ever died before, either.

"You don't know?" said Katherine, shocked.

Cecily frowned. "Know what? You mean about the disturbance earlier? Did the unicorns riot?"

"What? No? Why would they…?" Katherine asked in confusion. "Never mind, there's something I have to tell you. Something not good."

Worry crossed Cecily's face. "Well, out with it. I haven't heard anything from Mother. But I know she and the queen ran out of here in a rush two hours or so ago."

Biting her lip while holding back a sob, Katherine said, "Something's happened to Rose."

"What?" Cecily asked as Katherine sank down to the floor by the ladder and she sat down on the steps holding her hand with the jar at her feet. "What happened to Rose?"

"Her plane crashed and she died this morning," said Katherine numbly.

"Oh my god, Katy, that's horrible! How could something like that happen?" First shock appeared in her face with widened eyes, then tears began to roll down Cecily's cheeks.

Katherine shook her head. "I don't know. Your mom wasn't very forthcoming, and my mom pulled me out of school in hysterics. Kind of. Sort of. Well, I was already *outside* of school, but it doesn't matter now."

Cecily looked at her with tears streaming down her face. "I don't even think I want to know right now."

Katherine gave a shaky laugh. "Probably not."

"So are they sure? About Rose?" Cecily whispered. "Where is she now? I mean…her body?"

Katherine grimaced. "Not here. Not yet."

Cecily nodded. "A plane crash? Where was she going? How did it go down?"

Katherine looked over at her while wiping away a lone tear. "I was hoping you could help with that. You know, find out what happened. Those are questions I wondered about and…"

Katherine's voice trailed off as she was interrupted by Cecily's cell phone with a ringtone that Katherine had made her *promise* to change at least a hundred times. Cecily quickly grabbed it, looked at the screen, and turned off the harsh jingle.

"It could have been important."

"It wasn't," Cecily said while helping her stand. "I'll do anything I can to help."

"Thanks. I thought with you searching for clues we might find something," sniffed Katherine as she handed over the scarf in her hand.

"What do you mean?"

"I mean a plane crashed with a fully functioning crew and team of coven members. None of them should have died. Especially not Rose. And Derrick could control the freaking weather."

Cecily swallowed harshly. "So you think it wasn't an accident."

Katherine looked at her numbly. "It's hard to believe it was."

Cecily cut her off with wide eyes. "It's been six years, Katherine…you can't be thinking…"

"I wasn't," said Katherine harshly. "I wasn't. We know how he died. It was an accident. No matter what Mother says. But this…"

Katherine stood up and paced. "This can't be right."

"Does it feel wrong to you?" Cecily said, standing up to herself.

Katherine laughed cruelly. "Wrong? In the sense of a witch who can sniff out a lie?"

She turned back to see Cecily's arms crossed defensively.

Katherine's tone softened. "No, it doesn't. But you know me…my magic has always been useless for…you know…*useful* things."

Cecily raised an eyebrow. Not questioning. But cautious. If Katherine was in a mood, *more* of a mood anyway, she probably didn't want to provoke it.

"Like washing clothes?" Katherine offered weakly as a peace offering.

Cecily cracked a smile and chuckled. "Or dyeing your hair. Remember that time you went to school with snakes in your curls and bright orange hair?"

Katherine let a smile grace her face. "That was the night after that sleepover. They transferred from her to me. She was *lucky*. She only had one snake."

Cecily shook her head and they both broke out into laughter. Katherine's body released its tension. It was good to laugh with Cecily. Like today wasn't the worst and weirdest day in her life. Like Rose wasn't dead.

Her laughter slowed and a grim line appeared on her face. "I just... Cecily, the facts don't add up. The one and only time Rose leaves coven lands and protected territories and she's dead?"

Cecily sobered herself. "It is strange, I agree. What do you want to do?"

"Solve it."

"Solve what?" Cecily said, stepping forward, this time a hint of unease on her face.

Katherine gripped her hands. "Solve Rose's death. There's something they don't want us to know and something we must find out."

Cecily dropped her hands. "They? They who?"

Katherine flipped a hand in the air in irritation. "Someone. I don't know."

"Your mother?" Cecily asked softly.

"Yes!" Katherine blurted out before retracting just as quickly. "No! I don't know. I just know it can't be right."

"All right," Cecily said calmly. "Fine. Let's do what we can, then. There's no sense in speculating."

This time it was *Katherine* who crossed her arms defensively. "Speculating?"

"Would you prefer 'accusing your sworn queen and mother of keeping secrets'?"

The emphasis on the word "queen" was unmistakable.

Katherine grimaced. "No. But then again, that's why I came to you. You always make sense."

Cecily cracked a smile. "Of course I do."

Katherine sniffed. "So are you with me?"

"I'd hate to be against you," Cecily said wryly.

An indignant expression crossed Katherine's face before she saw the teasing smile on Cecily's.

"So first things first," Katherine's younger cousin said. "What's our first step?"

CHAPTER EIGHT

Katherine took a deep breath and fished something out of her pocket.

Handing it over to her cousin was hard, and even though it didn't even break the top ten lists of today's pretty awful deeds, it still hurt.

"The scarf is Rose's...*was* Rose's."

Her voice halted. Cecily looked on in compassion.

Katherine cleared her throat as she fought not to let emotion overtake her. "This was her favorite. She wore it all the time. Think you can make it work?"

"I'll do my best," whispered Cecily as she leaned over to give her cousin a hug and took the trailing fabric. Or at least she attempted to. Cecily soon found herself locked in Katherine's trembling arms, unable to see her cousin's face but feeling her body tremble.

When she put a hand on Katherine's back to soothe her, in the process letting her emphatic gifts venture out, Katherine was uneasy. Along the back of her head and up her spine Katherine could feel Cecily's emotional magic rising like a soothing blue mist from her hands as they made soothing circles. If she let it go on, just relaxed into it, then she knew her cousin's witches' gift would out her at ease. But she didn't want to be at ease, not to the mention the fact that she didn't like to get too close to anyone. And someone else touching her emotions, even if it was Cecily, was *too* close. So Katherine cleared her throat uncomfortably and stepped back.

Ashamed at her reticence but unwilling to explain herself or her actions, Katherine kept her face turned away with a sniff and a suspicious wipe of her eyes. The tear that she wouldn't acknowledge was her pain over Rose's death. The shame that lined the hunch of her shoulders was her own burden to bear. On top of the pain and the shame was anger. She was angry with Rose. She was angry with herself. The anger she could handle but she didn't want to explore the other emotions. Not yet. Not now. She had a job to do, and exploration of her feelings wasn't a part of that.

Crying won't help Rose. Actions will.

When Katherine turned back to look at Cecily, her face was clear, her eyes determined, and her voice held just a hint of husky sadness as she said, "Let's get to work, then."

They turned and went back into the storefront without another word. Cecily was unwilling to bring up the dark cloud that had hung over them like a forgotten ghoul since long before Rose's death. She and Katherine both knew that it would be ignored until the last possible moment. That was Katherine's de facto stance about most things that troubled her. From her homework to getting up at the crack of dawn to tend to Gestap's needs. Unfortunately, this dark and ominous cloud just seemed to grow and grow above her head. And like the appearance of her protectors earlier today, Katherine feared it would come to end in an explosive way.

"At least no one died today," she whispered to herself as she exited the basement storage room.

Or at least no one by *her* hand.

Katherine expected to walk into an airy room filled with sunlight and empty of customers. Only half of her expectation was accurate though. It was filled with sunlight and also filled with the presence of someone else. The thorn in her side stood right where they had ended their conversation minutes before and Katherine gritted her teeth as her fury returned.

Ethan just didn't get it, did he? She didn't want to see her ex-boyfriend, hear of him, or talk to him at all, especially not today. It didn't help that Cecily and Ethan had a separate relationship that Katherine did her best to ignore. It wasn't Cecily's fault that Ethan was her foster brother, but sometimes Katherine resented that he would show up at the most random times and there wasn't a damned thing she could say about it. He had the right to see his foster sister.

She held back a terse comment along the lines of, "What in the hell are you doing back here?"

Instead she settled for a polite but snarky, "What? Back to ruin my life some more?"

Ethan flinched. "Back to apologize."

"Apologize for what?" Cecily said absentmindedly as she focused her attention on the scarf running between her fingers.

She's probably checking for remnants of Rose's aura, Katherine thought as she glanced over at Cecily and back at Ethan. Apparently her cousin hadn't heard the shouting match between Katherine and her ex-boyfriend. Which suited Katherine just fine. She needed Cecily focused on one thing right now and that was on finding out everything she could about Rose's last day alive.

Meanwhile Ethan flicked his gaze from Rose to Katherine. He seemed to be asking Katherine a question with his eyes. Even though she hadn't spoken to him in months, she could tell that it was still there. That connection, that spark, whatever it was between them that had first brought them together was still there. Even if she didn't want it to be. That didn't mean she had to acknowledge it or make him feel better by giving him a sign of acknowledgement. She wasn't about to give him the satisfaction. Besides, Katherine didn't care what he said as long as he left. The sooner the better.

"Well?" Cecily said as she looked up and finally noticed the awkward silence.

Ethan blinked as if rising from a daze. Staring at Cecily, he said, "Well, what?"

Cecily gave an exasperated huff as she put her hands on her hips, scarf clenched in her right fist. "What are you here to apologize about?"

Her tone was miffed. As she had every right to be. She knew he hadn't done anything to offend her, and as far as Cecily was concerned Katherine hadn't spoken to Ethan in months. Up until a few minutes ago, that had been true.

Katherine watched Ethan carefully. She was tense, but the stiffness in her back and almost-clenched fists could have been a sign of anything. Really. Katherine would rather face something head-on than cry about it, and Cecily knew that. So the fact that she sometimes channeled her pain into anger was nothing new. But Ethan would know the difference. He'd already proved that. So she watched him as his troubled gaze turned back to her.

A tense few seconds passed.

Then Ethan murmured without taking his eyes off Katherine, "For a lot of things. But mostly for acting like an ass today."

Katherine's mouth twitched, but she said nothing.

Cecily noticed the awkward silence. Katherine could tell by the way her hand slipped from her hips to cross in front of her breasts in a defensive stance. Cecily's 'I'm on to you' look marched full-force into view with pursed lips, a tapping left foot, narrowed eyes, and crossed arms.

Fortunately, this time it was Katherine to the rescue. "He didn't know about Rose. Just like you didn't. And I kind of went off on him before."

"Oh?" Cecily said, blinking while slowly relaxing her tense shoulders.

Ethan took Katherine's words for what they were—a reprieve. Then he said, "Right. And I'm sorry about that, but there's something I came to do. I'll get it done and I'll leave. Alright?"

Katherine threw up her hands in frustration. "Whatever. Get it done."

Her cousin looked between Ethan and Katherine in confusion. Katherine could understand why. It wasn't like Cecily *knew* why they had broken up, she just knew Katherine avoided Ethan like the dickens usually and he gave her the same treatment. Which was harder than you'd think living in the same small town.

"What's going on?" Cecily said slowly. "Ethan, did you hear about Rose?"

He nodded in the affirmative while his frown moved into a thin, grim line.

He didn't look happy.

Well, he can take a number in the unhappy line today, Katherine thought, *because this sucks.*

She rubbed her brow in irritation and walked away to the other side of the room with her arms crossed. Anything to get away from Ethan. But she made sure to stay within hearing distance. Behind her, she heard Cecily say, "We were about to…"

Then Katherine got *very* interested in high-tailing her bum back toward them. She didn't want Cecily sharing anything with Ethan about her plans regarding Rose. Now or ever.

"Cecily," Katherine said hurriedly, "I'm sure we can handle it."

"Handle what?" Ethan said, looking back and forth between them.

Cecily raised an eyebrow and made a gesture to Katherine as if to say, 'be my guest'.

Katherine grimaced. "Does it matter what? It's not like you and Rose got along."

"And it's not as if I'm some heartless bastard, either," Ethan said with narrowed eyes. "If you need something, I'll do it."

"We don't," Katherine practically snarled.

"Whatever," Ethan said with a hurt note in his voice. "When you get around to the arrangements…I'll try to be there."

"Funeral arrangements?" said Katherine with a strange laugh. "Isn't it kind of early? Her body isn't even cold yet. We don't

 80

even know if they've *recovered* her remains. Fuck, it's not like you care anyway."

She was rambling. She knew it. They knew it. Rambling wasn't apart of Katherine's normal mindset.

Everyone stilled.

Cecily said, "That's not…"

"What he meant?" Katherine said stiffly.

Cecily squared her shoulders as she finished, "…necessarily true."

Katherine glared at her. Cecily continued on unflinching, "You know it and I know it."

"Maybe so," Katherine said stiffly. "But I stand by what I said. I don't, we don't, need him."

Cecily frowned and turned to Ethan with a look. "Maybe it really is time for you to go."

"Fair enough. I can see I'm not wanted here," he said, looking at Cecily. "So if you don't need me, Cecily…"

Cecily looked over at him in confusion. "For what?"

He raised an eyebrow. "*You* called *me*. Before Katherine got here. Remember?"

Meanwhile, Katherine was fuming and she was pretty sure if she didn't unclench her hands soon she'd be leaving marks on her arms. She was the type to bottle up her emotions and keep going—she wasn't going to collapse in a puddle, not Katherine Thompson. Unfortunately, that meant she was also one minute away from doing something she'd regret. Namely, calling down a few wind demons on her ex-boyfriend's ass.

Instead, she turned toward Cecily, keeping her back to Ethan, and made a 'get on with it' motion with her finger.

Cecily rolled her eyes as Katherine whispered, "Please".

Katherine would *love* to kick him out…again. But it hadn't worked so well last time, and Ethan was the thickheaded type that wouldn't do her bidding just because she asked. There had to be a reason. Well, what better reason to get him the hell out of her family's shop than 'oh, my sister died today and I hate your guts anyway'?

Out of the corner of her eye, a frustrated Katherine watched as Cecily rushed over to a side table and pushed a few of the dusty contents to the floor. One hit the old wood floors with a loud *crash*, but fortunately not the sound of shattering glass.

"Later," Cecily quickly said to Ethan over her shoulder while grabbing a brown paper bag and stuffing the contents of the jar inside. "It wasn't that important. Just remember to stop by and give Mr. Johnson this and tell him it's for his tea."

Ethan nodded, took the bag, turned away, and then turned back. Katherine waited with impatience sticking in her throat like a ball of gum threatening to choke her. She turned around fully to see what it was that was keeping him from leaving *this* time.

The guy's as stubborn and ornery as a goat, that's the only *reason*, she thought to herself. But when she got a look at his face, she felt her heart do a weird flip. Not romantically. Maybe anxiously? Yes, that was it.

Ethan's direct gaze was pinned on hers, but his mouth was in a bitter frown and he looked sad as he said, "I'm really, really sorry about Rose, Katerina. Let me know if there's anything you need."

Katherine nodded stiffly as Cecily walked back over to her and turned to face Ethan next to her as a good best friend should. She almost put a hand on Katherine's shoulder. Either to keep her friend from lunging at him or slapping him. Cecily probably wasn't sure which. Neither was Katherine.

'Katerina' had been his nickname for her when they were dating.

It was a nickname that still gave her butterflies and the insane desire to stab him thirty times with a knife for ruining her life.

When Katherine took a step forward, even she wasn't sure what she had planned. But Cecily quickly grabbed her hand as if to restrain her from going through with whatever urge it was. Cecily wasn't a mind-reader like Connor. She just knew her cousin really well. And she knew Katherine wasn't above stabbing someone. After she had conjured a knife from thin air and put a blade straight through the heart of a man twenty years her senior in sixth grade, there probably wasn't anything Cecily would put past her. To be fair he had it coming. He wasn't a man, he was a demon. And it was a queen's charge to kill demons. Katherine had a feeling that was the major reason humans hadn't decided to overthrow their queenly overlords, as numerous as they were compared to their witch brethren.

After all, the humans couldn't kill what they couldn't see and demons as well as all sorts of other nasty fae, higher and lower, were invisible to humans and their technology.

Ethan exited the shop unharmed. Cecily turned to her and leaned against the table in the center. They heard Ethan's motorcycle rev up in the parking lot before he rode off.

"You get the candles and chalk, I'll get the ingredients," Cecily said in the stretching silence.

"Still under the register?" Katherine asked as she fought to get a hold of herself.

"Yeah," said Cecily. She knew better than to comment on the topic of Ethan in Katherine's hearing distance. Add Rose's death on top of that, and it was turning out to be a very difficult morning.

An hour later, they had the incantation circle inscribed on the wooden floors in white chalk with candles set up on the pentagram points. It was an old-fashioned way to call up a vision, but currently the only way either Katherine or Cecily knew how to go about it without tapping into enough power to be visible for miles to another person searching through the power ley lines for a person with magic using their gifts. Whether they intended to harm that person or help them, Katherine wanted no part of another person with enough magic to seek out and find another miles away.

And right now, Katherine didn't want anyone knowing she was looking for Rose. Least of all her mother.

Cecily lit the candles one by one while leaning over from the center of the pentagram. "What exactly are we looking for?"

Katherine sat opposite her outside the circle. "First, for where Rose crashed. Tracing her aura from here shouldn't be a problem. Second, for whatever or whoever killed my sister."

"We suspect she was pretty far outside of town boundaries," said Cecily flatly. "That could be a tall order. But I'll try. Sourcing the location should be easy. *Should.* As long as there isn't something bigger or tougher hiding it."

Katherine nodded then teased, "Bigger or tougher? You're the toughest high school sophomore I know."

Cecily gave a strained chuckle.

As she blew out the match, Cecily continued, "Then let's focus on what we do know: the guardian has disappeared,

Derrick is on life support, and Rose is dead, but up until the moment she died, they were all together."

"Yes."

"Those auras together would have a distinct signature."

"Right," said Katherine, slow to catch on. "But how does that help? Oh! You can find the place they were last together and from there perhaps an imprint of their last moments?"

"Exactly," said Cecily.

Settling down with her legs crossed under her knees, Cecily opened her witches' gift —divination. She would try to *see* what had happened to Rose.

For Katherine, it was the most boring part of the ritual. Cecily had to go into a trance whenever she worked with her divination power and it was like watching a yoga master meditate. Katherine waited anxiously for twenty minutes as Cecily meditated and then Katherine got up and paced. When thirty minutes passed, she closed up the shop and started chopping up herbs. Anything to get rid of the boredom. Fortunately, it only took Cecily twenty minutes more to arise from the trance.

As she opened her eyes, Katherine walked over from where she was straightening the shelves with a hopeful expression on her face.

"Did you find anything?" she asked.

Unfortunately, the minute she asked the question Cecily went into a seizure.

Katherine dropped the glass jar full of sea anemones she'd been playing with and rushed to Cecily's side. Quickly she grabbed her from behind and turned her on her side with a firm push of her hands to keep any vomit from closing off her airway.

Soon the fits stopped and Cecily opened tired eyes.

Katherine gently helped her sit up.

"What did you see?"

"Black thorns," whispered Cecily before she became fully aware.

When Cecily's gaze snapped back into focus, she shook her head as if to dispel a dream. Leaning forward unsteadily, she tried to stand. She made it, but only with the help of Katherine's hand to balance her as she stood. Puzzled, Katherine looked up at her and stood as well.

Cecily looked shaken…as if this wasn't something she had done dozens of times before. Katherine had watched her. She would sometimes be disoriented, but she never snapped in and out of a conscious state like that. Never.

"Are you all right?"

Cecily shook her head. "I'll be fine." She was lying, Katherine could tell.

"You know what? Let me just go get a glass of water to clear my head."

Katherine watched as she went to the shop sink. As Cecily drank from the fountain, Katherine decided to try to dust the chalk off her jeans.

"What did you mean by black thorns?" Katherine asked.

Cecily turned her head slightly but kept her form bent over the sink. "What did you say?"

"I was asking about what you saw," Katherine.

Cecily turned around fully, a little pale. "You know I never remember everything I see. That's why I have you."

"Yeah," Katherine said while watching her cousin and friend carefully.

 86

The next moment pounding knocks on the door startled them both.

"We're closed," Katherine shouted at the door without turning around.

The knocking persisted.

Katherine went to the door and yanked it open, prepared to give the person a piece of her mind about disturbing her family in their time of grief.

The expression on the fire marshal's face stopped her cold.

Desperation was written in the stressed lines of his brow and the squint of his clear blue eyes. He held his rumpled hat with tight hands.

"Fire Marshal Ford, what can I do for you?" Katherine said.

"I can't get up to your house to see your sister, Katherine. Do you have any idea where she is?" he said tightly. "Rose was supposed to be at the town bridge an hour ago. The trolls are getting restless."

Quietly, Katherine said, "Rose died this morning, Fire Marshal."

He sucked in a tight breath as Cecily came over.

"Fire Marshal Ford," she said with a curious nod.

He glanced over at her and nodded before turning back to Katherine. "I didn't know, Katherine. Your family has my sympathies."

"Thank you," she said, prepared to smile and close the door.

He still didn't budge except to wipe a sweaty brow with a cloth that had seen better days…and way too many oil changes.

As she eased the door closed, he stuck his foot out in a hurry.

"But there's still a problem to be handled." he said with a lick of his lips. "I wouldn't normally be so forward, but we need Rose. And if she has passed, then we need you."

"Me?" Katherine said, staring at him as if he were crazy.

Everyone in town knew that if you needed anything political, you went to Rose or the queen. If you needed anything magical, you stayed five miles away from Katherine with a couple of buildings in between for good measure.

He sighed. "Yes." She could feel the reluctance in his tone and tried not to take offense.

"This is really the duty of the heir. Never the queen," he continued.

"Ever?" said Katherine sarcastically.

He glared at her. "Ever. But don't fear—your powers aren't needed here. Just your heritage and your ears."

Katherine's eyebrows rose to her hairline as she fought to keep a neutral expression on her face...and failed. He was kidding, right?

He didn't flinch.

"Could it wait until tomorrow?" Katherine asked, expecting an affirmative.

"No," he said. "Depressed trolls aren't really something you want to leave to their own devices. And they'll only listen to a witch of the Thompson line."

Katherine blinked at him, wondering if she had heard him right. Depressed. *Trolls*. Could trolls even *get* depressed?

She cleared her throat and turned to Cecily who shrugged. Katherine was hoping for her cousin to say something along the lines of, 'Yes, he's clearly insane and I'll call the police'. Instead her cousin threw her to the wolves.

"Rose did a lot of *odd* things for the town," Cecily said.

Then it dawned on Katherine. Rose was dead. Rose was the heir. With the heir dead, the next person in line inherited this small dipshit town in the middle of nowhere. Horror overtook her face with the realization that the next person in line was *her*.

She was now Queen Bee of Sandersville.

CHAPTER NINE

Her jaw dropped as she stared at Cecily, and all Katherine could say was, "My life's officially gone to hell now."

Being the good friend and cousin that she was, Cecily quickly took over. To the fire marshal, she said, "The bridge, you said?"

He nodded.

"We'll be right over," Cecily said firmly while taking the door in her hand.

The fire marshal didn't look too comfortable with that. He probably didn't want his only possible solution slipping away.

Cecily's voice turned to butter. "There's only one bridge in town, Fire Marshal. Only five minutes to get there. We just need to close up the shop quickly and phone Katherine's mom to let her know we'll handle it."

He brightened at that. It was good to keep the queen informed. "Then I'll see you two ladies in ten minutes."

He backed away and Cecily closed the door behind him.

Katherine turned to her cousin and grabbed her shoulders. "Did he say what I thought he said? What the hell am I supposed to do with depressed trolls?"

"We'll find out when we get there," Cecily said firmly while handing her the pink cell phone. "Now call your mother and tell her we're on the way to the bridge while I clean up this mess."

As Cecily walked away, Katherine said, "Well, she did say I was to 'take care' of things while she dealt with Rose's death."

As she swept, Cecily said, "That makes sense. If the heir dies, the next one needs to get up to speed, and *fast*. What better way than throwing the fat into the fire?"

Catching Katherine's expression, she quickly said, "So to speak."

Katherine gave her a weak smile and dialed her mother. Aunt Sarah answered.

Their conversation was short, sweet and to the point: "Don't mess this up."

With a *click* the conversation was cut off, and Katherine was left listening to an empty line. Her aunt sure had a way with words. Katherine let out a harsh sigh. "We'll take care of this but I need to find out what happened to Rose. What did you mean by 'black thorn'?"

Cecily avoided her eyes. "I wish I knew. I'm sorry. Sometimes my visions are just symbols, or flashes of events."

Katherine noted internally that this was the second excuse Cecily had given in regards to what she saw. First it had been that she didn't remember. Now it was she only saw a flash of it. Which was true?

"So you *saw* a black thorn?" Katherine persisted.

"I think so. But I'm not sure," Cecily said, hurrying to finish. "Why don't we lock up here, go see about the trolls, and come back in ten minutes to finish what we started?"

Katherine grimaced, but she could see that it was a good plan. Besides, if Cecily wanted to really analyze the vision without rushing, they had a better chance of getting some clear results.

Aloud, Katherine said, "We did promise to get over there quickly."

"And it shouldn't take too long," Cecily answered with a nod as she swung open the shop door with the keys in her left hand.

As they headed out the door, Katherine got into the driver's side of her car as she thought of something that was bothering her. Looking over at Cecily while putting the gear into reverse, she said, "Trolls? Really?"

Cecily shrugged.

Katherine groaned. "I really wish today would go back to being normal."

"Don't we all."

Katherine looked at her cousin again. She was acting strangely. But today was full of the strange, the morbid, and the depressing. And it was only mid-afternoon. She could only handle so much at once. Putting the SUV in reverse, she drove out to the bridge, hoping whatever it was happened to be a simple fix.

Maybe the trolls needed some herbs from the shop?

She tried to think about what a troll would eat. Couldn't figure out a bloody thing. A crypto-zoologist she was not.

As she parked on the town side of the gorge which divided Lancashire County from Buckstone County next door, she asked Cecily, "Are trolls vegetarians or omnivores?"

Cecily unfastened her seatbelt and got out. "Have you seen their teeth?"

Katherine shook her head.

"They're as pointed as a barracuda's. Definitely meat eaters."

"Great," grumbled Katherine while wrapping her scarf more tightly around her neck and stuffing her hands in her pockets. It was starting to snow.

They rushed to the edge of the bridge, where two police cars had the entrance blocked off. Peering to the other side, Katherine saw police tape cordoning off the other entrance as well. Quickly she and Cecily got out of the car, searching for the man in charge. When she spotted the fire marshal who had been knocking on the door of their shop minutes before, she plastered a smile on her face and walked over.

To the fire marshal, she asked, "What's going on?"

He shouted back over the wailing that started echoing up from the gorge, "Trolls are on strike."

"Strike? I thought you said they were depressed!"

"They're depressed *and* they decided to protest."

"Fuck me," said Katherine. "Why? What are they protesting?"

He grimaced. "Something about some ritual that people forgot about. Supposed to have started this morning."

"Ritual?"

He grimaced. "You'll see."

Katherine sighed. "Am I supposed to go down there alone?"

"No," said the fire marshal, "two of the uniforms will escort you."

She nodded and headed toward the embankment.

"Word to the wise," he called out.

She looked back over her shoulder to see the fire marshal and Cecily standing next to him.

"Bring a guardian next time."

Katherine didn't comment, but she thought, *Having a guardian didn't seem to help my sister this morning.*

With the uniformed police officers behind her, she climbed down the side of the gorge using the steel ladder embedded in the wall. One of the officers offered to float her down with his witches' gift, but she didn't *know* him. He could be excellent or completely sucky at using his powers. And she would rather not end up flat as a pancake on the bottom of the gorge, thank you very much. As she climbed down, she occasionally looked back up at the steel suspension bridge that hovered overhead. She never looked down. If she did she knew she'd be too petrified to move, and then she'd be stuck clinging to a ladder rung.

After twenty minutes of bitter cold, stinging winds, and occasional small rocks tumbling past her, Katherine made it to the bottom and promptly stuffed her gloveless hands into her coat pockets, wishing all the while that her witch's gift dealt with heat or fire or lava. Anything that would warm her up, really.

Turning around to look for the trolls, she saw nothing but large boulders in an empty riverbed all around her. The officers soon made it down next to her. One said, "They're over there, ma'am."

He was pointing west.

"Okay, then," she said, trying to sound brave.

She was not easily frightened, but you try entering the lair of a pack of depressed trolls without being a tiny bit nervous. As she walked forward, the eerie wailing ceased. Not a sound echoed in the gorge except the footfalls of Katherine and the two policemen by her side as well as the occasional tumbling rock. One of the officers walked in front of her to shine his light when they started weaving around large boulders.

They came around the last boulder to find an open area directly underneath the bridge and a pack of trolls staring them down. Six, to be exact. Of all different sizes too. One was as big as the car. Another as tiny as a house cat. And four more ranged between them in various sizes. All different colors. Some with tusks curving out of their jaws. Others with small, serrated teeth emerging from their crooked jawlines. Every single one of them was crying.

Taken aback, Katherine walked forward slowly with an officer on either side.

When Katherine and the officers got within fifteen feet of them, the trolls started howling. And they didn't stop even when she stood staring at them less than a stone's throw away.

Finally Katherine couldn't take it anymore. "Stop!"

They halted. Tears flowed.

"What's the matter with you lot?" she asked in exasperation.

The trolls looked at one another in uncertainty.

Helpfully, she added, "I'm the daughter of the Queen of Sandersville. The new heir. I'm here to help."

One of the trolls, the smallest said, "We know."

She sighed in relief. "So you *can* talk."

"Of course we can *talk*," said one of the medium-sized ones in an outraged voice.

Katherine held up a hand. "Don't get your panties in a bunch. I've been waiting for you to stop wailing for nearly ten minutes. After ten minutes of *that*, anyone would question your ability to speak."

The littlest one sniffed. "Well, we can. We just chose not to."

Curious, Katherine asked, "What did you mean you *knew* who I was?"

The trolls looked at each other and back at her. "The blood has passed. The power has shifted."

That didn't answer her question. She tried another as she looked from one to the other. "What do you want?"

The second smallest one rose up from where it crouched on its hind legs with its ears flapping. "The ceremony. The great ceremony was supposed to commence. You did not come."

"I wasn't *supposed* to come. My sister was."

"That one died. You were supposed to come," pointed out the large one.

"'That one' was my *sister*," said Katherine tightly.

"Yes, we know," they all said.

Katherine was getting a headache.

"How is the ceremony commenced?"

They looked at her and back at each other.

The little one spoke up again, "We sing."

"Yes, we sing!" said another one, "and you enjoy."

Katherine stared at him with a disbelieving expression on her face. Abruptly she turned around. "I'm out of here."

She didn't get two steps before the wailing started up again and a uniformed officer—the warlock—was in her face.

"Get out of my way," snarled a fed-up Katherine.

"Wait, please," he pleaded, "you don't understand."

"I understand perfectly," she said. "They want me to listen to them sing. I don't have time for this nonsense."

The troll wails were doing more than giving her a migraine. They reverberated through her like a pounding pulse that went through the rock and the earth surrounding them, as well. She needed to get out of here.

The officer stopped backing up and pointed to the small rocks falling all around them. "Look!"

She stopped, looked at the gorge wall and then back at him. "Look at what?"

"The rocks are falling for a reason. It's because the walls are trembling. Why is the gorge trembling? It's because of the *trolls*. Their wailing gets stronger by the minute. The stronger the wail, the louder the pulse."

Katherine grabbed the front of his shirt. "Why should I care?"

She growled and then said, "Forget that question. At least tell me if that's why you have the bridge closed."

"Yes, but it's not a simple as that. We're not doing this *just* because they're upset," said the other officer watching her.

She threw up her hands. "Then why?"

"It's because it's the fact that they're upset which will ultimately cause the bridge to fall. They're deliberately trying to bring the gorge down around all of their ears. Their depression is driving them to this. To suicide."

Katherine looked at him and then looked back at the trolls. Their tears still flowed.

"How?" Katherine scoffed.

"The reverberations from the howls are destabilizing all of the earth around us. It won't be long before the ridge crumbles and the earth softens and folds in on itself. Taking them and the gorge bridge with it."

"Their wailing is strong enough to do that?" she asked, uncertain.

"Stronger with every passing minute," one of the officers confirmed.

"And you're saying if I listen to them sing, they'll stop."

"Not only that, but their singing has the opposite effect of the wails. It reinforces the bridge and the structure around it."

"Singing good. Wailing bad," said Katherine with some irony.

The warlock officer nodded. "Once a year, one of the Sandersville Thompson line comes down here and listens to them sing. Praises their strength and their dedication to the bridge. They're happy. We're happy. The bridge doesn't collapse into the gorge. Got it?"

Weakly, Katherine said, "Got it."

"So make nice and show them you appreciate them please," he said tightly.

The new heir to the Sandersville throne turned around, pasted a smile on her face, and sat on the hard ground to listen to a pack of six trolls serenade her for two hours with traditional troll folk music.

CHAPTER TEN

As Katherine stood up politely at the conclusion, the smallest of the trolls came up to her and presented her with a small rock that he had picked up along the way. As he walked forward in skips and jumps she watched the round piece of rock he juggled in his hand. She wasn't nervous. Just attentive. With each step the rock took on a luminescence that was otherworldly. By his last step, it glowed a white so bright that it was like moonlight. With a brilliant smile on his face, the troll that came no higher than her knee presented the glowing rock to her with both hands upheld as if he were giving her the greatest gift on Earth.

It was a glowing *rock*. But she didn't say that.

His ears twitched back and forth as he smiled and waited for her to accept the token.

The bared teeth were actually more gruesome than friendly. Katherine could see bloody bits of whatever the troll had for breakfast still stuck in his teeth. Still she accepted the rock with a smile of her own.

"Thank you," she said as she held the smooth stone in her cupped hands. She wasn't sure what to do with it besides hold it.

Fortunately, he didn't seem to expect much.

"You are the new blood heir. We hear your words. We feel your blood. We will serve you," he said excitedly. "We will keep the bridge whole and the people will cross quickly."

"Thank you. Thank you for your song and for keeping the bridge whole. The people who cross are very grateful," she said. She didn't think the people who commuted over the bridge cared one lick about the trolls' efforts *now*, but she knew they would the minute their access to the town from their farms across the bridge was cut off. It was human nature. Ignore something that worked well and complain the minute it broke.

When nothing more was forthcoming from the smallest troll, she glanced over at the warlock officer. He wasn't paying her the least mind. She turned back to the troll only to see him bow and start walking backwards to his group of fellow trolls.

As he left, Katherine smiled and bowed to the group. The trolls each bowed back solemnly. For every troll that bowed to her, Katherine bowed to it. There were only four of them. The problem was that they kept bowing over and over again. She could quickly see this becoming a diplomatic incident on the level of the great drug scandal four years back. That particular incident stuck in her mind, because it was the closest the town came to a drug raid with sirens blazing, not to mention that fact that two buildings on the main street of Sandersville had ended up on fire and a group of faeries arrested for dealing in unstable moon nectar.

Scary stuff then. Even scarier now, because if she messed this up, the responsibility wasn't on her mother's head. It was on *hers*.

Fortunately, an officer behind her cleared his throat before she could commit a troll cultural faux pas.

She bowed once again and said, "Excuse me," as she smoothly turned around.

"They won't stop bowing until you leave," he said.

"Great," Katherine said as she refrained from telling the smiling officer off for not speaking up sooner. "Let's go now."

She gave one more bow and followed the warlock officer out of the rocky home of the trolls and back to the steel ladder that led up out of the gorge.

Seeing the steel ladder from the base, Katherine groaned aloud. If it had taken her close to a half-hour to climb down, it would take at least triple that to climb back up.

The radio on the warlock officer's shoulder beeped then silenced.

He turned to her and said, "You know, it's courtesy for a warlock to escort his future queen from point A to point B. Seeing as I didn't get to see you down the gorge wall, I figure it's my duty to see you back up."

With something akin to undying gratitude pasted on her face, Katherine accepted the warlock officer's offer to fly her up the incline with an utterly sincere, "Bless you." Her butt hurt and her legs ached. There was no way she was climbing up the ladder the same way she had come down.

He called in a platform of solid air. She stepped onto it with no hesitation.

Before she could ascend, the radio on his shoulder beeped again.

He responded, "Officer Matthews."

The fire marshal responded, "We've got a situation, Todd. You almost through there?"

"Just finishing up," Officer Matthews responded while looking at Katherine. "Sending Katherine back up to the top now."

"Good. Out," said the fire marshal.

Katherine grimaced. "What kind of situation?"

"Not sure yet," Officer Matthews replied with a grin. "But can't be too much sadder than depressed trolls."

She got the joke. She just didn't see why it was amusing.

"Right," said Katherine while looking pointedly up the gorge walls.

He lifted her through the air without further comment.

Reaching the top, she stepped off the air platform and took the hand of the human officer waiting to assist her.

Dropping his hand when her feet where firmly planted on the ground, she walked stiff-legged to the SUV she had liberated only to see Cecily with a bag of Cheetos in hand, a road map spread out over the SUV hood, and her pink cell phone floating over a divination grid that made a map of the constellations look like child's play.

Katherine couldn't help the fact that her legs shaking awkwardly on the way over. Her butt hurt like hell from sitting on a dry riverbed of rocks for two hours and her legs had fallen asleep a half-hour into the presentation.

When she reached them, the fire marshal said in sympathy, "The trolls probably wouldn't have minded if you got up and moved around."

"No, but if she had they would have expected her to start dancing along with them," said Cecily.

Katherine raised an eyebrow. "You saw their attempts at interpretive dance?"

Cecily nodded at the pair of binoculars clutched in the fire marshal's hand.

"Yep, it wasn't that bad," said her cousin while sucking the cheese dust off of her fingers and waving her other hand to push the divination grid over until its gold dots hovered above the road map.

"Speak for yourself," said Katherine, peering at her cousin's work. "What's that?"

"We got a call in," said the fire marshal.

"From the gods?" said Katherine, looking at Cecily's divination grid with a raised eyebrow.

Cecily shook her head. "Worse—the dark faerie have called a meeting. They want you, your mother, and the Coven Council to call a new witches' conclave before the high moon rises tonight."

Katherine stared in astonishment. "What in the world for?"

Cecily asked, "Is it the dark faerie or their king that is heading this pact?"

Katherine raised an eyebrow. That was a good question. It was important to know who was leaving who in this endeavor.

"From what I heard, it's their king alone who wants a new queen," the fire marshal said.

Katherine asked, "Is Ceidian drunk again?"

"Most likely," said Cecily.

"Undoubtedly," agreed the fire marshal.

Their expressions were serious. Katherine sighed. "But we still need to go and explain to His drunken Majesty for the second time in a quarter that the dark faerie have no jurisdiction in the forests west of Sandersville, right?"

"Yes," said Cecily.

"Uh-huh," said the fire marshal.

"Lovely."

"There's one more problem," Cecily said before her phone rang.

Before Katherine could say a word, Cecily quickly answered the call and said, "Thank the gods. Did you find out—what? No."

Katherine raised an eyebrow, wondering who Cecily was on the phone with.

"Where?" Cecily quickly said into the phone while pointing a ready finger at the hovering golden grid.

"You're sure?" she continued while moving her finger quickly and making the dots hover over three points on the road map. "Okay, got it."

Cecily snapped the phone closed.

"Who was that?" Katherine asked.

"Ethan," Cecily answered while she focused on the road map, missing the grimace that passed over Katherine's face.

"What did he want?" Katherine asked.

"He was doing me a favor," Cecily said. "He went to the human representative's office to find out where the faerie are meeting today."

"What would the editor of the town's newspaper know about the faerie?" Katherine asked.

The fire marshal looked over at Katherine and said, "He has a name—Jarvis Copper. Jarvis has his fingers in every pie in this town. Which is why your mother works closely with him."

"Really?" said Katherine dryly. "I thought it was because he demanded the least outrageous kickbacks and kept all the moon nectar, opium, and blood dealers in line."

"There's that also," admitted Cecily. "Which is why he would know *exactly* where the faerie dealing grounds are on a daily basis. You can't buy and sell if you don't know where the product is."

"If it were up to me, I would have run them out of town years ago," said Katherine.

"Good thing it wasn't," said the fire marshal, a tad too derisively to Katherine's liking.

When she turned to glare at him, he stared back with stern eyes. "I don't know what your mother has explained about your responsibilities or town negotiations, but you need to get up to speed fast."

Katherine opened and closed her mouth. She wasn't about to compete against him. Mainly because she knew squat. Rose was the heir. Rose went to council meetings. Katherine took care of Gestap and had planned her way out of this podunk town since freshman year. But it was hard to stare into his eyes and not shrink back as the wisdom of twenty-plus years on the force of the town fire brigade stared back. That was *a lot* of experience when you considered the fact that he frequently dealt with fire salamanders and survived.

Finally the fire marshal cleared his throat and continued.

"Kicking out the dealers would have done nothing but create a void that no one would have wanted to deal with. Your mother was right to keep them around and keep them in check," pointed out the fire marshal. "The lamias would have nowhere to go for blood, the selkies would go crazy so far from the sea without the opium, and don't get me started on the moon nectar effect."

Cecily and Katherine looked at each other and shuddered. The fire marshal had a point. The inferno on Main Street four years back hadn't exactly been an accident. The moon nectar had dried up and chaos had ensued.

Finally Katherine said a bit uncertainly, "Calling for a new queen will only get the same refusals for him then. *No one* in their right minds would let him control unicorn territory."

"And yet he persists," the fire marshal said in a grave tone. "It would behoove a true heir to find out why."

Katherine got the point. The faerie king wasn't dumb. Proud, but not stupid. There had to be a reason to be this forceful about the issue, especially when he was so determined that he would not only seek to unseat his queen for a second time, but also risk her wrath on the day of her daughter's death...a day for mourning.

"Perhaps it's time I have a talk with the faerie king," Katherine said finally.

"Perhaps it is," the fire marshal said with a hint of approval in his voice.

Turning to Cecily, Katherine asked, "So what did Human Representative Copper tell Ethan? Where can we find him?"

If the fire marshal noted her proper respect for the human representative's title, he didn't say anything. Still, she could feel his hard stare easing up and even relaxing in the same manner she knew what time it was without looking at a clock or at the position of the stars. There were some benefits to being the minor daughter of a blood family. Exploring the world around her without actually using any of the five traditional senses given to human and coven alike was one of them. She could use a sixth sense to do so.

"He gave us the location of the highest rates of faerie phone traffic today," said Cecily while busily pushing the divination grid into various sections of the map. "Here, here, and here."

The golden dots now hovered in bursts of concentrated light above specific points in the map. Points as far apart on the map as they could be without being in the jurisdiction of another queen.

But that wasn't Katherine's focus now. She was still hung up on the 'phone traffic' part of Cecily's comment.

"He what? We're tapping people's phones now?" said Katherine.

"Not tapping," huffed the fire marshal, "merely tracking activity. As you well know, the faerie are addicted to their phones. Won't go anywhere without them. Which works to our advantage. It's our only way this late in the game to know where the dark faerie gatherings will be tonight.

Katherine's respect for his twenty years in the fire brigade went down a notch. Was this really the way they were handling this? She felt it was little invasive for the situation; the faerie king and his people didn't pose a threat to the community, after all. Just her mother's reign…and peace of mind.

"I'll be sure to bring that up when people start mentioning their fourth amendment rights. I don't suppose you have a warrant?" said Katherine.

The fire marshal grunted.

"Right. I thought not," said Katherine. "Why couldn't we just ask one of the faerie in the local market where they're going tonight?"

"Because the king of the dark faerie is a dick, as you know. He's put a ban of silence on all of his people. Any of them talk to us and they get burned," said Cecily while looking up from the maps in frustration. "We're almost out of time. These locations are at the far end of the county line in opposite directions."

"Your cousin's right," said the fire marshal. "It'll take an hour and a half easy to get to any of these points in addition to the tracking through the woods you'll have to do on foot."

"Fantastic," muttered Katherine.

Then her eyes narrowed in suspicion. "Wait, what do you mean 'you'? I said I'd talk to him—I didn't say I'd go out in the middle of nowhere to do so. Beside I just took care of those whiny trolls. It's your *job* to keep the dark faerie in line."

"And it's your job as heir to keep the power-drunk dark faerie from ransacking the unicorn lands and the human farms. All of which are part of the territory this faerie king so desperately wants to grab," said the fire marshal calmly.

"Who knows what nefarious plans he has in store," Cecily helpfully added.

Katherine angrily glared at both of them with her hands on her hips. They were ganging up on her. When both innocently looked over at her, Katherine rolled her eyes and threw up her hands.

"Being heir sucks," said Katherine. No one disagreed.

But it was her job now. Her sister wasn't even in the ground yet, and things were going to hell in a hand basket. With a sigh,

Katherine put her hands on the map and carefully traced the routes. She looked from one to the other. "How am I supposed to be in three places at once?"

"You aren't," said the fire marshal. "We'll go to the first drop zone together. If the king isn't there, we'll go to the next."

Cecily nodded. "We just need to get there before the sun sets and their power amps up. So, depending on the time, we'll have to choose the second or third spot carefully."

Cecily, Katherine, and the fire marshal eyed the map in speculation.

Katherine said, "Then let's go to the forest grove first. The faerie king loves his picnics and the gods know there's no better place."

"I'll round up my men," said the fire marshal, walking off with his radio at the ready.

"Ready to be the heir of Sandersville?" said Cecily softly with her hand on Katherine's shoulder.

"I better be," said Katherine. "Because if I mess this up, you're next in line."

Cecily blinked. "Yeah, let's make sure that doesn't happen. I couldn't imagine a job I want less."

"Hey," sniped Katherine.

Cecily grinned and rolled up the road map.

CHAPTER ELEVEN

The fire marshal rounded up his men and spoke to them tersely. Before Katherine could join the conversation, they had scattered to the trucks in the area.

"Let's move out!" said the fire marshal.

"Coming right up," one officer said to Katherine, "I'll drive your SUV if you want to ride with the fire marshal, ma'am."

She tossed him her keys. "Have at it."

Exchanging anxious but excited glances, Katherine and Cecily piled into the red truck with the fire marshal. With the fire marshal's truck in the lead, they whipped along the roads within the southern branch of town.

Katherine gritted her teeth when she saw traffic, or what passed as traffic in Sandersville—pickup trucks parked directly in the road by owners too lazy to go around back, and a horse-drawn carriage complete with a Minotaur acting as driver-cum-bodyguard. Cecily's mouth curdled into a frown as she recognized the Minotaur. They had nothing against the servant and everything against its owner. In a town so small that everyone knew everyone else, when disagreements happened, grudges were kept forever. And in the case of raven-haired and blue-eyed Lisa Anne Renner, scion of the oldest and wealthiest Sandersville family, that grudge ran deep for the Thompson cousins.

Lisa Anne was a bitch, plain and simple, and her family owned the largest tobacco farms on this side of South Georgia. Which meant she was a rich bitch. Fortunately Katherine and Cecily didn't have time to so much as roll down the window and speak to their small-town nemesis before the fire marshal turned on his sirens and cleared the intersection with a few furious blasts of his horn. As they sped through, Katherine's eyes caught Lisa Anne's. For a moment their gazes locked, and then Lisa turned away and the truck raced through the main thoroughfare. Once the fire marshal reached the edge of the main block's limits, he sped up along the empty roads bordered by empty fields to either side.

They were going to Margaret's Grove. Named after the fourth queen to rule Sandersville, it was the place where the town held the annual barbeque and picnic in the summer. A beautiful clearing surrounded on all sides by cedar trees, it was also the perfect setting for a faerie drug deal or a faerie king's attempt to rise to power.

The ride over was silent. Their arrival was anything but.

They piled out of the car into an empty field and the officers along for the ride piled out of the cars like a S.W.A.T. team. Moving with a precision that she didn't know they were capable of they swept the field as a unit.

III

Katherine asked, "Are they all caring detectors?"

"The human officers are," said the fire marshal beside her while his eyes swept over the field for any sign of disturbance, his binoculars at the ready in his hands.

"And the warlock officers will use their senses," said Katherine softly as she paced away from the cars, opening her own magic to the auras in the field.

She heard the fire marshal quickly protest, "You should stay here."

But Cecily hushed him. "You wanted her here to stop the uprising. Well, she's here. Let her work."

Then Katherine stopped paying attention to the humans and witches in the area and focused on the power that flowed through the grove. The reason Queen Margaret had chosen this grove to have the annual barbeque and picnic was simple. She was smart. There were certain points in the world where it was easy to cross over from the human realm to the other realm. All witches were taught to look for those points. They could be sources of great power and great evil. To counteract the bad juju that a source portal attracted, you needed good vibes. There were various ways to attract the goodness of the world. The white witches, a sectarian group of coven society that most witches referred to as 'power vegans' behind their backs, believed in cultivating a sense of harmony with nature and their fellow beings. That worked...as long as the dark witches weren't down the street sacrificing goats and calling up demons.

Queen Margaret had decided to take a few examples from the white witches and a little from the dark witches in an ingenious move that made Katherine crack a smile to this day. She held a barbeque for the whole town with free food, free drinks, and entertainment for even the grumpiest of residents. Everyone gathered on the same spot by the queen's command. Light and dark. Fae, witch, and human. And they all enjoyed the festivities. That much goodwill in one spot was enough to imbue the entire grove with good karma for the year. And it was renewed year after year. Everyone knew why the queen held the town barbeque the second time around. But no one complained. Free food and free beer turned even the angry centaurs to the queen's side. If there was one thing all the residents of Sandersville agreed upon, it was that the queens of Sandersville knew how to throw a party.

Now Katherine used that goodwill for her own purposes. Muttering a quick prayer to Hecate, the mother of witches, she opened her powers to the divide between the realms around her.

Like a curtain being drawn aside, the door was revealed. It glowed in streaks of gold as she walked forward purposely to the outlined veil. She noticed the warlocks around her stop and stare, but they didn't interfere. They knew better than to cast their own spells when a witch was at work. The divide wasn't a two-way street. It went to different dimensions and different worlds, realms just for the fae and realms just for the gods. She hadn't been to either. Her mother wouldn't let her. But she could peek inside once, just to be sure the faerie hadn't decided to hide on the other side until their search party left.

Katherine didn't think they would be. It wasn't King Ceidian's style to hide out in plain sight. But then again he seemed to get crazier by the day. She had a sneaking suspicion that he was imbibing some of the moon nectar he sold. Which wouldn't be good for either side—witch or fae. But it wouldn't kill them. The humans, on the other hand, would be up the creek without a paddle if the faerie king were a drug dealer hooked on his own product.

Pushing aside the golden veil between the realms felt like touching a gossamer curtain. Light and airy, with a spark of magic that tingled along her fingertips. She was careful not to step between the realms, though. It was enough to look on the other side and see what was there. She knew from her lessons that the faerie couldn't move very far from their jump point from one realm to the other. If they did they might end up jumping into Brazil instead of North America.

To her disappointment, the fields on the other side were an empty mirror image of where she now stood. Dropping the veil, she stepped back and turned around. "There's nothing here," she shouted to the fire marshal.

He shouted to his officers, "Pack up, men, we've got two hours of sunlight left."

Katherine cursed as she hurtled to the trucks with the officers around her flat-out running to either side.

As they got back into the truck, she said, "Stupid winter. Why is it already closing in on dusk at three o'clock in the afternoon? Ridiculous!"

"Can't do nothing about that," said the fire marshal, taking out the road map and crossing out where they now stood. "Where to next?"

"We have two hours?" said Katherine.

"Less," said Cecily. "We need to get there and convince Ceidian before his power is at its peak with the end of dusk. We can't afford to cross him without your mother on our side, on his turf, *and* at night."

Katherine groaned. "Where's Mother when we need her?"

"I spoke with her guardians," said the fire marshal. "Because of the horrific death of Rose, she needs to be consecrated in the ground immediately. The queen is on her way to the burial grounds to start the ritual now."

Katherine's stomach dipped at the mention of Rose's name.

"Immediately?" she said, horrified. "But I'm not there."

Cecily gripped her hand hard. "If she doesn't do it now, Rose's gifts won't pass to you, and any witch within ten miles might take on that power. Your mother knows that. You know that. And the town can't risk a takeover by a power-hungry witch."

Katherine grimaced. She knew it was true. The Thompson line protected their subjects. But there were witches out there who made a hobby of gobbling up towns and counties in power-grabs, all in order to challenge the high queen for supremacy. It happened every century.

"We're not going to let Sandersville be a prize in some trumped up witch's bid for power," Katherine said firmly. "Let's go take care of Ceidian. Mother will take care of Rose."

Cecily nodded, pride at her cousin's strength written on her face.

Katherine looked at the map and hoped her luck would last.

"The waterfall's on the county line. We'll go there next," she said.

The fire marshal radioed his men. "Head for the waterfalls. Marks—you and your team split from us a half-mile out from the falls. Go up the back roads and make sure there isn't something nasty waiting for us. The queen's heir, the demon hunter's daughter, and I will go up the front with Officer Matthews and his partner."

The men radioed their agreements.

The fire marshal whistled and put the truck into gear. "Let's hope this is the one, ladies."

Katherine pursed her mouth and said nothing. The nervous butterflies in the pit of her stomach were doing all the talking now.

Forty minutes of dusty roads, hairpin turns, and one mowed-down rabbit later, they had made it across town, through the tunnels, and out to the base of the mountain path that led to the town's claim to fame: the Sandersville waterfalls. A picturesque scene of iridescent rocks, purple waterfalls, and hundreds of dark faerie met her gaze. They were waiting for her.

She got out of the car slowly. As her booted foot hit the dirt beneath the truck tires, she almost flinched and dove back into the car. The earth was vibrating with the power of the dark faerie. Shuddering, she put her foot back on the truck ledge and looked over at Cecily. "Stay in the car."

Her cousin was already scooting from the middle seat to come out behind her.

"No," protested Cecily.

"Listen to me," urged Katherine. "Something's not right. You said it yourself—you're next in line. If something happened to you *and* me, there's no way Mother could raise a proper heir to take over in time. You need to stay in the car."

Cecily didn't pout. Just barely. But her mouth descended into a dark frown. But then she looked out over the dark faerie gathered in a half-circle just a few feet out of the range of the truck's headlights. Not that the distance mattered. They were all glowing like fireflies at night.

Cecily swallowed deeply. "All right."

"Here," said the fire marshal from the other side of the truck.

Cecily turned around in the seat and Katherine saw him give her the keys.

"If things go hairy, hit reverse and push that pedal," said the fire marshal. "Get out of here as fast as you can."

"If things get hairy, I doubt it'll matter how fast I can drive," said Cecily. But she palmed the ring of keys anyway.

Looking back over at Katherine, she said, "I'm going to study the auras from here. See if I can help. Keep an eye on your texts, will you?"

Katherine nodded.

As she prepared to close the door on her side, Cecily said from behind her, "And Katherine?"

The new queen bee of Sandersville turned a head to her younger cousin as she waited patiently for her to speak.

Finally Cecily swallowed and said, "Be careful, will you? I *really* don't want to be heir to the throne. I have enough problems of my own."

Katherine cracked a grin at what she thought was a joke, but deep inside something felt wrong about the last statement. She couldn't put her finger on it, though, and she didn't have time to question Cecily right now anyway. She stepped out of the truck and closed the door behind her.

She and the fire marshal walked around the truck. Side-by-side they walked up the incline in order to talk the insane king of the dark faerie out of starting a war he couldn't possibly win...and deposing her mother while he was at it.

CHAPTER TWELVE

As they walked forward, the silent dark faerie mass parted like the red sea upon their approach and Katherine looked around. She saw massive faerie eyes with the telltale second ring of power surrounding each iris. They looked a lot like those mutant dolls with the sparkly irises filled with a wide spectrum of colors. Except for the fact that these faerie were anything but doll-like.

They stood at least six-feet-tall with human-like appearances. But all of them were frighteningly skinny. Katherine frowned. 'Skinny' wasn't really the right word for it.

More like desiccated husks, she thought to herself.

She had never seen the faerie as they were now. Their flesh was barely raised from their bones. No hint of hair emerged from their heads. Their eyes, almost too big for their pale forms, were huge, and their wings were desiccated like dried husks on their shoulders.

 118

Katherine felt a sadness like she had never known rock through her.

"How could this be?" she whispered to the fire marshal beside her.

He looked around with his mouth pursed in distaste and his baton at the ready. "It's gotten worse."

"Worse? This is more than *worse*," hissed Katherine. "Look at them! They're all hooked on moon nectar. They're pale shadows of their former selves."

The fire marshal was silent and then he carefully chose his words. "It's the monarch's prerogative to lead his or her people in the ways they see fit."

"Yeah, well, maybe this monarch isn't *fit* to lead his people," Katherine whispered as they continued their march forward, surrounded on all sides by vacant and bleary eyes.

"And yet they stand as they do now. With no protest," the fire marshal said.

"What are you saying?" Katherine asked. "That my mother allowed this when she should have intervened?"

"No, I'm saying that there is no one who *could* intervene in this situation. A king's kingdom is own."

"Well, he's in my mother's queendom, and we don't play games like that here," Katherine said with steel in her voice.

The fire marshal's eyes flickered over to her face, but he said not a word further until they were moments before the ledge on which the faerie king perched.

Then he spoke with a caution. "Be careful of your words here, Katherine Thompson. Your mother has no jurisdiction over how the King of the Dark Faerie leads his people. She may set the rules between interactions of the fae, witches, and humans, but make no mistake, Ceidian rules his domain."

And then there was no more time for chatter. Katherine looked away from the fire marshal to see the dark faerie king lounging on a giant boulder of volcanic rock. Unlike his people surrounding them, he was not wasted by the effects of moon nectar. No, his skin glowed like alabaster while his long, dark hair fell to his knees. His purple orbs, encased with a ring of blue, shone with eager attention, and his body was clearly in its prime with sleek muscles and iridescent wings that reminded Katherine of a mix between a butterfly's width and a dragonfly's texture.

Then he spoke. His voice was gravelly by nature and it was like listening to rolling thunder on a moonlight night.

"Ah, so the queen's spawn has come?" said the reclining king.

Katherine's back went up as she snapped, "Queen's spawn? Who do you think you are?"

Turning to the fire marshal, she said in disbelief, "Who does he think he is?"

"Easy, Katherine," urged the fire marshal while putting a cautious hand on her shoulder.

Turning to the dark faerie king, the fire marshal said, "I'd treat the queen's heir with a little more respect."

The faerie lounging around their king hissed at the fire marshal.

"She deserves no respect. A weak daughter for a weak queen," Ceidian responded.

Katherine jerked her shoulder from the fire marshal's grip and strode forward. "My mother isn't weak. And from the look of the faerie surrounding me, you are the one who deserves no respect. Look what you have done to your people."

The dark faerie king sat up abruptly. "What *I* have done? My people suffer because of your mother."

"Come again?" said Katherine.

He narrowed his glowing eyes in anger as a tic appeared at the corner of his mouth. "Do not jest with me. I do not find it amusing, on this night or any other."

Katherine crossed her arms and stared at him. He was serious. "All right, lay it straight down then."

For a moment the angry monarch tapped his fingers subtlety on the rocky throne. Then he did as she asked: he laid it out. "The moon nectar my subjects have ingested? It is not our brew."

Katherine stared at him. "What in the devil's name are you talking about?"

That was impossible. The drug was harvested by faerie laborers and banned countrywide from production by anyone else. Not that no one else could do it, but that no one else was willing to *try*.

The dark faerie king stood up and snapped his fingers. A faerie with red rings around her purple eyes stumbled forward out of the masses. Katherine watched her. She looked weaker than most. Her arms were like twigs and her ribs showed clearly below the simple breast band she wore.

She stumbled to her king and fell to her knees.

With an angry jerk of his arm, the dark faerie king turned her head to Katherine's eyes.

"Look, look at her!" he demanded.

Unease rolled through Katherine, but she didn't look away.

"What am I looking for?" she said unsteadily.

"The luster of her skin is gone, the strength that runs through her veins has run dry. She is a pale imitation of what she once was," said Ceidian softly. "This. This is the work of spiked moon nectar. Vile stuff that kills instead of satiates the hunger of my people."

Katherine looked from the shell of a female faerie back up to the vibrant king. Quietly she said, "One could say just as easily that one week of constant drug use could be the cause."

She didn't have direct experience, but she wasn't a fool, either. She knew the risks. Everyone did.

"And one could just as easily say one taste does not make an individual an addict," the king said while his hand tightened imperceptibly on his subject's chin. "I've known Madeleine my entire life, rocked her babes to sleep, and helped her settle into a new life—she is no constant user. Once was enough to make her into this shell of a person. Once was enough to drain her dry."

Katherine watched the claws of his sharpened nails pierce the skin of the woman's chin ever so slightly. Blood began to seep out around the corners of each point. Ceidian didn't seem to notice. Neither did the woman. Both were in another world. Ceidian, one crafted of misery and regret. Madeleine, one of opiates and unearthly desires.

Katherine rocked back on her heels as she absorbed that information. She was careful to keep her questions moderate, but she couldn't keep the shock from her voice. "How is this true? How do you know?"

The dark faerie king stared at her disdainfully. "Because she is not the only one affected. This tainted concoction is driving my people to death."

"I understand your concern here, but it's your fault. Your people are hooked on moon nectar because of *you*." That wasn't very charitable, but then again she wasn't feeling very nice at the moment. The sun was sinking ever lower and this discussion was spiraling into a debate with no end. She felt for Ceidian, she did. But she needed a resolution *now*, before night took hold. Not at dawn when he finally agreed that his people's addiction to moon nectar was no fault of any other species or person but himself.

"I provided them with a taste. A small bite. Nothing more," he cried. "But this is an intoxication that they cannot break. It blinds them with need and drives for more. They will die if they continue like this."

"Then stop them," Katherine urged.

"I've tried," said Ceidian darkly. "But I cannot stop the influx of these tainted goods. My people need a taste of the moon nectar to survive on these lands. But the moon nectar of old has gone. It replaced by something I do not know. Nor do I know where they originated from, but I know they have desecrated my people and their bond with the land. Which is why I've called for your mother's abdication. She allows this filth into her territory. Allowed my people to be fooled by tainted goods. Now she must pay the price. A queen who does not protect her territory shall not rule."

Katherine's stomach dropped completely.

"Now hold on a minute," urged the fire marshal.

The king turned furious eyes to the fire marshal. "This has gone on long enough. We've tried your way, now we will try mine. A new queen shall rule. One who will root out this evil! One who will destroy the clan that has wreaked this havoc!"

Katherine's eyes twitched. "What if I can find the source? End it for you?"

"You?" scoffed the dark faerie king. "You are a child."

"Besides," said Ceidian, "I already know the source, and by the fall of the sun I will kill the were-peacocks for their shame."

Katherine jumped. "You just said you don't know where the tainted goods are coming from!"

"That doesn't mean I don't know who's distributing them," said the king softly. "And they will rue the day they brought these tainted goods to my kingdom."

Katherine turned to the fire marshal in desperation. His eyes looked void of hope.

She turned back to the dark faerie king. "You're talking about starting a war."

"No," said Ceidian with a smile. "The war started long ago. I merely mean to finish one."

Horror built up in Katherine's throat, because she knew he was dead serious.

Just as she stepped forward to speak again, the sound of the truck horn blasted through the serene sound of the waterfalls behind them. Katherine turned to see her cousin frantically laying on the horn and waving at her. Katherine shook her head and prepared to get out her cell phone to tell Cecily now wasn't the best time. Although really Cecily should know that already. When Cecily opened the truck door and looked like she was about to jump out of the cab, Katherine quickly turned and ran toward her.

Over her shoulder, she shouted to the king, "I'll be back in like half a second."

Rushing to the truck, she opened it and stood in the doorway jam.

"What?" Katherine said.

Cecily said, "We've got more problems."

Katherine looked down at her watch. "Worse than a faerie king dead-set on wiping out a clan of were-peacocks in less than half an hour?"

Cecily put a hand over the watch. "Maybe. I don't know. How do you feel about blood ceremonies?"

Katherine looked at her. "What in the hell are you talking about?"

"I was scouting the faerie from here. Whatever they drank wasn't intended to give them a high," Cecily said. "In fact, it gave them a disease."

"Run that by me one more time?" Katherine said.

"The faerie people are *sick*," stressed Cecily.

"Yeah, I know," said Katherine while looking through the windshield at those who stood closest to them. It was perfectly clear that something was wrong with them.

"No, I don't think you do," Cecily said in exasperation.

"They're not just physically addicted, they're dying."

Katherine's eyes were still trained on the mass of individuals gathered below their king. "That's not possible."

She didn't bother turning around to debate the point. There was nothing to debate.

Still Katherine said aloud, "The faerie people don't get sick. They don't get headaches or ailments. They are in perfect health from the day they arrive to the day they leave."

"I didn't say they were dying, Katherine," Cecily pointed out. "I said they're ill. Just look at them for a moment. All of the

125

signs are there, Katherine. The skin, the hair, and even their posture. Those aren't the signs of being high from moon nectar. That is a people being drained of their life forces."

Katherine looked around her. Hesitant. It was one of the most outlandish theories she had yet.

"I want to believe you. I really do," Katherine said. "But you have no proof and we've been here less than fifteen minutes. How can you diagnose an entire race as sick when you haven't spoken to one of them?"

Cecily sat back and irritably pushed away a clump of curly hair that had descended into her eyes. "Their auras," she said flatly.

"Will give you a hint of their powers and emotional status," ventured Katherine, "Nothing more."

"But you don't get it, Katherine," Cecily insisted. "Faerie are *different*. Their entire being is caught up in their magic and sense of self. Strip them of their powers and you're stripping them of a life force. Strip a witch of her magic and she becomes human. She doesn't wither and die."

"That's not proven," countered Katherine.

Cecily glared at her cousin.

Katherine amended her statement. "All right, the faerie part isn't proven."

"What more proof do you need than what is standing right before you?" countered Cecily.

When Katherine didn't answer Cecily let an irritated growl release from her throat and made a move as to throw open the driver's side door. Katherine leaned over to hastily grab her arm before she could exit the cab.

"Wait!" Katherine said desperately. "Just wait a moment."

Cecily turned back to her cousin with defiant eyes. "If you want to know if the cause and effect is true, just ask their king."

"And sign our death warrants? I don't think so," said Katherine shakily. "His people are immortal. Everyone knows that."

Cecily opened her mouth to argue and Katherine shook her arm impatiently. "Don't you get it? He would fight to maintain the reputation. It is legend that nothing can kill a faerie warrior. To see them taken down by addiction would be incalculable."

"He would rather let his people die slowly?" Cecily said.

"I think," Katherine said with a deep breath. "He would rather find a way to end the supply without making it known that the effects at work are other than just being an opiate haze."

Slowly Cecily removed her arm from Katherine's grip and rubbed circulation back into the offended flesh.

Katherine barely noticed as she sat back in the passenger's seat. "So we know two things. Ceidian's right. And the moon nectar given to his people is spiked in some way."

Cecily nodded. "Because the faerie have been taking it since arrival within the lands of the original colonies with no problem like this. They don't become addicted; *they* are generally the addiction for unwary mortals. Their recreational opiate has become their death sentence."

"And somehow that same nectar is now not only addictive to them but...fatal?" Katherine wondered.

Cecily grimaced. "It's not the drug this time. I think it's the holes in their auras."

Katherine raised curious eyebrows. "Do tell."

"Picture glowing white bodies," Cecily said as she shifted uncomfortably in her seat. "In a dark field. Each of the bodies is filled with a luminescent white sheen of power. Now imagine that power being drained from their bodies into the night sky."

"Is that what you're seeing?" Horror laced Katherine's voice.

"More or less," Cecily said with a rub of her eyes. "Some of the faerie are better off than others and the king is not affected at all, but they all are losing their gifts, which means they're losing the essence of who they are."

"Poppycock," Katherine cursed as she sat back against the headrest with a *thump*. "And I thought the day couldn't get any worse."

She believed Cecily. How could she not? The evidence was right before them. And the faerie king was bordering on madness. Not because he feared losing his people to an opiate. But because he feared death itself. What was war when an individual had nothing to lose?

Katherine looked back at her. "Where is the power going?"

"I don't know," was the disappointing answer Cecily gave.

"Then how about a source? How does someone infect an entire population and drain their powers without other people noticing? *Lots* of other people?"

"You mean besides preying on the mild addiction they all suffer from, turning it into an all-out epidemic, and siphoning off the powers as the result? The entire combination makes it look like something less complex than it is. Even Ceidian seems to think his people are merely suffering from the effects of a drug spike," Cecily said a little too smugly for Katherine's taste.

"What kind of tampering would break down their shielding and open up their power cores to something like this? What could they have possibly done to the moon nectar to cause all of this?" Katherine felt like pulling out her hair.

"Do I look like a biologist to you?"

At this point Katherine was talking to herself. "And who would benefit from it?"

Cecily sighed. "I hate to point it out, but certain denizens of the western forests near Sandersville have been really agitated lately."

"Agitated?" said Katherine flatly.

Cecily shrugged. "That's one way to put it."

Katherine took in a deep breath and let it out. "You really think the were-peacocks had something to do with this?"

"With how chummy they've been with the unicorns lately?" Cecily said. "I wouldn't put it past them and I think we'd be fools not to find out," Cecily replied.

"Any chance you're wrong?" Katherine said slowly.

"About sixty-percent," Cecily replied straightforwardly. "But I read their auras. This is no joke. Regardless of whether or not it's the moon nectar that's the cause, we need to track down who is stealing their powers, and fast."

"Because a people's lives are at stake?" Katherine said a little uncertainly.

Cecily shook her head until her earrings jingled. "Because this is nasty stuff. I'd hate to see it spread to other fae or witches. That is one trouble we don't need and every species, regardless of ability has a weakness. *This* just exploits the faerie. What happens when it's the selkies or the dragons or the lamia or the kiltern or anything else, really?"

Katherine held up a hand. "All right, I get it. Grave magnitude. Much bad juju."

Cecily gave a chuckle. "That's an understatement. This is like wading through a sticky mass of dark death and illness. I so need a shower now."

"Okay, so what do you suggest?"

"This is so far out of my field, Katy," Cecily said. "Sorry."

Katherine grimaced. "Yours and mine both."

They turned to look out on the gathered fae. Katherine took a deep breath and exited of the truck. "Thanks for the heads-up."

"You're welcome," she heard her cousin say as she took a deep breath, squared her shoulders, and walked out once more into the faerie mass. It was like being surrounded by once-beautiful corpses.

Katherine gave a small shudder that she kept from her face when she looked back to check on Cecily, who she could see was in the driver's seat with her nose pressed to the window.

Then things got interesting.

Katherine walked back to the fire marshal. Her stomach in twists because she knew the sun would set in ten minutes.

She prepared to speak with him and he said, "I already know."

She looked at him curiously.

He said tersely, "Diseased fae is a hell of surprise. Never thought I'd hear that combination."

"How did you know?" asked Katherine.

He tapped the radio on his shoulder. "There's another radio on in the car."

"Any bright ideas, then?" she asked the fire marshal.

"One," he said reluctantly. "Offer him an antidote."

"You've got one?"

"We'll get one," he said darkly.

She swallowed and looked over at the dark faerie king. Ceidian was inhumanly beautiful, but she had the gut feeling that he was inhumanly scared, as well. Scared for his people.

Stepping forward, she looked directly in his eyes. Searching for something. Compassion. Fear. Anything she could connect with. She found nothing. But that didn't mean it wasn't there.

"What if I could offer you an antidote? To cure your people's ill?"

"There is no cure for addiction," he said after a moment.

She raised her chin. "Addiction, no. Pestilence, yes. We believe that there's more to the moon nectar than meets the eye."

"And you're basing this assumption on what?" he snarled. "The child in the truck's supposition?"

She narrowed her eyes.

"Yes, I heard the whole thing," Ceidian said.

"Then call it a really good premonition if it'll make you feel better," snarled Katherine.

"Then you know that *child* is a future prophet," said the fire marshal at the same time.

Katherine nodded in agreement. "Cecily may be young, but her visions are always true. Let me prove it to you. Give us two days, a sample of the tainted moon nectar, and we'll get your antidote."

The king traced a thoughtful finger on his lips. "And I suppose you want me to stay here and watch my people waste away while you do?"

Katherine said, "Forty-eight hours won't kill you, and it won't make a difference if you assault the unicorns now or then. Give us a chance and your people might recover."

The king looked at her with darkened eyes. He said nothing for a moment.

"You have twelve hours," he said slowly.

Katherine didn't protest. It was better than nothing.

He gestured for a withering fae to give a stoppered flask to the fire marshal. He took it gingerly. They would have to get samples of the nectar to the nearest bio-facility as soon as possible, though.

"Thank you, Your Majesty." She turned to leave.

"Wait," Ceidian commanded.

Katherine turned to look back at him with wariness.

"You will take Nestor with you," said Ceidian, waving a subject forward. "He will be my eyes and ears."

Katherine's lips twisted as she fought back a knee-jerk reaction. Instead, she politely said, "That's not necessary."

"I insist," the king snarled. He wasn't backing down.

"Very well," she said with reluctance. She didn't have a choice.

Out of the crowd Nestor came forward, and Katherine's jaw dropped.

CHAPTER THIRTEEN

This time her knee-jerk reaction won out.

Katherine Thompson opened her mouth in order to protest and protest hard. There was no way in hell this man she knew well, or *thought* she knew well, was the king's subject. He couldn't be. There must be some mistake. If there wasn't, the man had some explaining to do. Even if it *was* a mistake, the guy still had some explaining to do. She couldn't take her eyes off of him as he turned a neutral gaze on her and took a step forward, not sure yet what she planned to do, but knowing that it might involve two felonies and a misdemeanor.

Fortunately, before she could take more than a step she was halted. The fire marshal nearly cut off the blood circulating in her arm when he gripped her hand so hard she squeaked.

She shut her mouth with a snap. She said not a word. Not in front of the faerie king and certainly not in front of his subjects.

Nestor came up on the other side of the fire marshal. To his credit, he didn't look happy about being called from his hiding place among his fae brethren. Katherine couldn't blame him. The faerie king had effectively blown his cover with one command. A command that, if he was true fae, he could not disobey.

Katherine's mouth was suddenly dry. She couldn't speak.

Fire Marshal Ford spoke for them both. "Nestor, I'm Fire Marshal Ford. This is Katherine Thompson, the Queen of Sandersville's daughter."

"We've met," said Nestor coolly.

That was enough to unlock her silence.

Katherine's eyes were flint ready to spark a fire. "We've *met*? We *dated* for six months. What the hell, Ethan?"

She was beside herself with fury. Ethan stood there in jeans and a T-shirt as calm as a cucumber with his hands in his pockets as he stood encircled by fae and facing down his irate former girlfriend. A look of boredom was on his face.

"Is there a problem?" asked Ceidian from his throne upon the rock.

Katherine turned to him. "Yes, there is."

"No," said the fire marshal shortly.

But Ceidian's gaze was fixed on one person. Katherine.

"Katherine Thompson?" he purred her name as a question.

Katherine's face twitched. If she didn't know any better, she'd say the king was enjoying this. She turned her head slowly and took in Nestor-cum-Ethan or whatever he was choosing to call himself. Nestor didn't blink, but for a moment the ring of power around both of his irises faded and for a few seconds she saw the eyes she had come to know. The eyes of Ethan Hawke, the normal but slightly magical mortal she had once loved. His eyes asked her for leniency. She felt like punching him in the jaw, but she'd give him time to explain. Besides if she hurt him in front of his court, Ceidian wouldn't take that nicely. Oh no, she could hear him declaring war on not just the unicorns but the witches, as well. On top of his case for political impeachment against her mother that is.

Katherine nodded slightly to Ethan. He nodded back. Almost imperceptible unless you stared hard at both before they turned to look back at the king. They had an agreement—they would discuss their personal issues later. Guy-to-girl. But for now the king's will needed to be done. To save numerous lives.

"No, my lord," said Nestor smoothly. "I was just introducing myself to the witch queen's representatives."

"Very well," said Ceidian in a tone that clearly questioned why they were still there.

Katherine stalked back to the truck where Cecily waited in the driver's seat with wide eyes.

"Is that...my *brother*?" said Cecily. "What's Ethan doing here?"

"You got me," grouched Katherine. "But we're going to find out. Mind sitting in the back?"

Cecily was still staring at her brother, who was approaching the passenger's side door.

"Cecily?"

"What? Oh...uh...no," Cecily said as she pulled down the middle seat and scrambled into the back. Katherine slid into the driver's seat and pushed the middle seat up. Ethan got in on her right. Fire Marshal Ford got in and cranked the engine on her left. For five minutes there was silence as they slowly backed out of view of the waterfall and the car turned around to get back on the road.

"Ethan Walker," said Cecily, "what in the world were you doing out there with the fae?"

Ethan sighed. "I live with them, Cecily."

"What?" his sister said, astonished. "Since when?"

"Since your bitch of a mother, my foster mother, kicked me out," he said. "I had nowhere else to go. No job until two months ago, and no one would rent a place to stay to an underage kid with barely a hundred bucks to his name."

"You could have stayed with us," said Katherine tightly.

Ethan laughed grimly. "Oh yeah, that would go over so well with your mother. The queen hates me."

"She doesn't *hate* you," said Katherine tightly. "She just doesn't…"

"Like me?" finished Ethan.

Katherine crossed her arm and looked to the left across Fire Marshal Ford and out the driver's side window.

"So what now?" she asked. "You're spying for the fae?"

"I serve the king on a few select missions in exchange for room and safety among the faerie," said Ethan with a hollow ring in his voice. "Out of all of the things he's asked me to do, this actually isn't so bad."

Cecily sat forward from the backseat. "Did you even *see* the human representative? Or was that just a lie?"

Ethan twisted around in his seat and his arm brushed Katherine's as he did so. She felt a pleasant tinge of heat, but she forced it down ruthlessly. Ethan was the enemy…and a douche.

Ethan said gripped his foster sister's hand and said to her, "I wouldn't lie to you, Cecily. I did what I could to help you out.

Informing you where the king was most likely to be. Even *I* didn't know. He made his mind up at the last minute."

"Oh," said his foster sister softly.

Katherine snorted in disgust. "Don't be so quick to forgive him, Cecily. He's hiding more than he's telling. I can *feel* it."

Ethan turned to her. "You're a precognitive now, Katherine?"

The question was said so derisively that she almost slapped him. Instead she asked, "So what's up with the ring of power in your eye? Don't tell me you're faerie, as well?"

"Do you see wings on my back?"

"There are all kinds of fae," Katherine shot back.

"Well, there's your answer," said Ethan tiredly. "You know, Katherine, if you asked the right questions, maybe I wouldn't do so much hiding."

"The right questions?" repeated Katherine while turning to him with fire in her eyes. "Here's a question. Why are you such an asshole?"

"All right, *enough*," snapped Fire Marshal Ford. "You two sit back and please stop bickering. You, boy, is it Ethan or is it Nestor?"

Ethan said stiffly, "It's both, sir. My full name is Ethan Nestor."

"Ethan it is, then," said the fire marshal. "Now, we need to get that antidote, but first we need to know what's in the moon nectar that's causing this disease-like reaction."

Cecily piped up from the backseat. "Then we'd better go to the shop. I have everything there to study it."

"Not a bio lab?" asked Katherine curiously.

"No time," said Cecily while fiddling with her phone. "Human containment rules would put it in isolation for at least twenty-four hours. We have less than half of that to find the source and the cure."

"Right," said Katherine.

"Ethan, you're not going to have any problem with that, are you?" said the fire marshal in a serious tone.

Katherine tensed.

"No, sir," replied Ethan. "I'm only here to report on your activity. Not to hinder your investigation. For real. If you can find out what's causing this wasting sickness among the fae, you'd be doing the king a huge favor."

Her shoulders relaxed, but she still felt tense. Not because of Ethan, but because the weight of this task was on her. *She* had to find the cure, or her mother's throne would be in peril.

Cecily gripped Katherine's shoulder and squeezed. "We'll get this done."

"I hope so," Katherine whispered back to her.

Then she turned to the fire marshal firmly and said, "So we're heading to the shop, then?"

He nodded. "We'll stop there to see what we can find out."

Katherine heard a catch in his voice.

"Where you planning to go somewhere else?" she asked.

She noted the fire marshal's knuckles whiten as he tightened a hand on the steering wheel. "I'm afraid there might be some truth to the faerie king's claims of were-peacock involvement. They've been secretive about recent shipments into town. I think it's time we find out what they had coming in on those late night trucks."

Katherine and Ethan exchanged glances involuntarily.

"Ethan needs to stay with the moon nectar," Katherine volunteered. "So why don't you and I check out the were-peacocks?"

The fire marshal nodded. "We'll drop these two off first."

They were back at the shop in half an hour flat. They'd burned through a few red lights to do it and turned a few corners that made Katherine think she was going to die at the base of a cliff, but they made it. Turning to Cecily, Katherine reached over the seat to give her the vial. "We'll be back in an hour no matter what."

Cecily nodded and got out through the back door. Ethan followed her into the darkness as she opened the shop's front door.

Katherine leaned over to grab the open door as she scooted to take Ethan's spot. As she was swinging the door closed, Ethan caught the door in a firm grip.

She looked over at him, startled.

Expressions warred on his face. But fear won out.

"Be careful out there," Ethan said. "They may be were-peacocks, but they fight dirty."

She nodded, unsure what else to say.

He let go of the door and she slammed it closed.

The fire marshal put their car into gear and headed off into the night. They hadn't even gone five miles before his radio beeped. He picked it up and said, "This is Fire Marshal Ford, who's on this line?"

"The queen wishes to speak with her daughter," said a male voice.

"Transferring," Fire Marshal Ford said.

He touched a button on his radio to halt the conversation and turned the knob on the handheld radio sitting on the dashboard.

To Katherine he said, "It's live."

She picked up the handheld and pressed the button down. "Hey, Mom."

"Katherine," said the queen's voice in relief. "Where are you?"

"En route to the were-peacock mansion, Mom," she said. "Did you hear what Ceidian wanted?"

"No," said the queen, "but I'm afraid I know *why* he wants it."

"What do you mean?" asked Katherine.

"Tell Fire Marshall Ford to bring you home," the queen implored. "I've already sent a team for Cecily at the shop."

"How did you know?" said Katherine.

"I called her," the stressed and tired queen pointed out, "but that's not important now. We have the antidote for the fae."

"Shouldn't we take it directly to Ceidian, then?"

"No, and I'll explain why when you come home."

"Right, okay," said Katherine as she watched the fire marshal turn the truck around in one smooth move.

"And honey?" said her mother.

"Yes?"

"Rose is laid out for her ritual," said her mother with sorrow in her voice. "I thought you should know before you walked into the house."

Katherine was glad her mother had told her. As the fire marshal made a quick left turn to take them up a side street and over to the queen's house, her mind flashed back to the last time she'd seen a coven member put to rest. It had been her father almost ten years ago. She didn't remember the ceremony all that well, but she did remember the smells. The room had been filled with blooming flowers in the tradition of their coven's burial style. She knew from lessons that only close family members had attended the ritual and the ceremony always started at the witch or warlock's home. She didn't think Aunt Sarah had been there...and Cecily had been too young. Which left Rose and Katherine to comfort their grieving mother. Except for a woman with hair as a light as a field of flaxen wheat. Katherine didn't remembered who she was. Just the impression of gravity that emanated from her. She'd never seen that woman again, and she didn't have the heart to ask her mother who she was. Their father had been the love of her life and now she was laying to rest her oldest child in the same home. It would be too much for some people. But not for a queen, not for her mother. She would get through this. Katherine would make sure of it. If it was last thing she did, she would see her mother through the burial and the trials that seemed to piling one on top of the other like the ravens of old legend, spiritual birds that brought warnings of foreboding times.

"Well, it can't get much worse than your daughter dying," Katherine said darkly, "so bring it on. I will handle it."

"What was that?" the fire marshal said sharply.

"I said that whatever happens I will handle it," Katherine said while looking over at him with a glint in her eye. "It will be handled it. Everything will be all right. My mother will be fine."

Katherine wasn't sure who she was trying to convince more, herself or the fire marshal. Thankfully he didn't say anything else as they pulled off the main street and toward the lonely road that led to her home. Soon they turned onto the same driveway that she had peeled out of at top speed just a few hours ago, and her mind drifted back to the upcoming ceremony. The final ceremony for her sister. So vibrant in life and so very silent in death.

Katherine knew, as all cove members knew, that they had to lay to rest Rose's spirit before laying to rest her body. Which meant that Rose's recovered remains were currently laid out somewhere in the house. If she had died of natural causes Katherine would have assumed she was in her bed. But she didn't know. How could she know? Her stomach roiled as she thought about it. About something marring Rose's perfect face, about scratches from plane shrapnel on her arms, about torn flesh on Rose's chest.

Then she shook her head firmly and told herself, *It's not true. None of it. Rose is dead, yes. But her body is fine. It will be sanctified and I'm going to say goodbye.*

Katherine closed her eyes in grief as she said, "I guess I'll be able to see her put to rest after all."

She just hoped she was ready to say goodbye.

"Yes, you will," said the queen.

"We should be there in ten minutes, Mother."

"I'll see you then." The radio went silent.

They pulled up to the front of the queen's gates to see one guard at the entrance. He peered into their car and waved them on through. As they piled out of the truck, Katherine noticed a curious thing: a total lack of guardians except one at the gate and two in the house. She felt unease and rushed up the steps. Where was her mother's protection team?

Opening the door with a shout that she couldn't help, Katherine called out, "Mom!"

"I'm here," answered the queen almost immediately. Her voice was coming from the formal dining room. Katherine turned to the right and swiftly covered the distance.

She walked through the French doors to see her mother seated at the table with her aunt at her right hand and a very unusual guest seated on top of the table. Literally crouching with plumed feathers spread and beady eyes focused on her entrance was someone she'd never thought she'd see in her mother's house.

Because if the Queen of Sandersville was disdainful of anything, it was the seedy underbelly that made up the darkness of their small town. Yes, she did business with them, the were-peacock cadre being the worst of the lot that Katherine knew about, but it always on neutral grounds. But tonight it was in her home. Before her stood the head of the largest mafia of fae in all of Sandersville.

CHAPTER FOURTEEN

The lord of the were-peacocks stood in full transformation on top of the chestnut dining room table. He was twice the size of a normal peacock, with brilliant plumage and iridescent feathers. Vivid purple, iridescent blues, and eye-catching yellow and orange met her gaze. My, he was beautiful. Beautiful and a noble pain in the ass, as she knew from experience. While it was openly said that the king of the faerie wanted to overthrow the queen, the dark whispers around town made no secret of the fact that the were-peacock was so prideful that he didn't want to merely dethrone the reigning queen, but also thought he was good enough to bed her as well.

Him.

A were-changeling…bedding a provincial queen. It was laughable. Even if the queen wasn't her mother and she didn't object to the notion based on familial attachment, it was still a completely absurd concept. Witches, especially royal witches, didn't have sex with the least of the fae.

My demon-hunting aunt notwithstanding, Katherine thought with a shudder. She suspected there was more than one reason her aunt refused to talk about the man who was Cecily's father, the man they had never met, the man she had raised Cecily in secret with for the first of year of her life, and the man who Katherine was quite sure she'd never have a chance to figure out.

It didn't matter, though. What mattered was what was in front her.

He turned his small head to her as she walked into the room in shock. Shocked to see him here in her home. And irritation that her mother, as usual, was two steps ahead of her daughter. Katherine had hoped that she was ahead of the game this time. But it wasn't to be.

"Mother, what's going on?"

The queen turned to her daughter. "Mr. Thomas LaCroix was just about to tell us that, dear."

Katherine wasn't quite sure how that would be possible. Since Mr. LaCroix now stood incapable of speech with that sharp beak.

But as if he understand her mother's words—and Katherine knew weres could understand human speech even if most couldn't manage to communicate in the sounds necessary to mimic it, the peacock on top of the table leapt forward—directly at Katherine. Before she could get a face full of the feathered thirty-pound peacock, he transformed into a man. A naked man. Mr. LaCroix landed on the floor in a crouch with his skin drenched in the slimy liquid that all were-folk produced after a transformation and looked up at her with oddly crafty eyes. She hadn't expected an imbecile, a love-swept idiot maybe, but not an imbecile. One didn't become the lord of any of the were-fae without first rising to the occasion, and since the positions weren't hereditary, that meant he risen through the ranks by cunning, strength, and wit.

She didn't like this were-lord's gaze, however. It was assessing and presumptive all at the same time. As much as Katherine liked to make fun of Gestap's manners, he'd taught quite bit about the fae communities under a witch queen's rules. So she was very much aware that the were-community aligned themselves with a very much different code of moral conduct than the coven did. Hell, most fae were more comfortable in the nude than their coven and human brethren. Nevertheless, across fae lines one thing remained the same: a mutual respect for the culture of others. Which meant that the Mr. LaCroix's heavy stare in his nude form was quite rude from where Katherine was standing. He was in her home, and beholden by the etiquette and standards of coven society. If this meeting had been located in his home she would have acknowledged him with a head tilt and looked aside politely without a word.

But they weren't and she didn't. It didn't help that she didn't like him or his attitude towards her mother, either.

"Can I help you with something?" said Katherine, unbowed.

"Perhaps," the lord said. Then he stood and Katherine was forced to stand rigid and stare him down. Never mind the fact that the top of her head barely reached his collarbone and she couldn't help that she was blushing.

Out of the corner of her eye she saw her mother frown and start to move from around the table. But she stopped, not at her aunt's behest as Katherine would have surmised, but by the actions of whoever was coming up behind Katherine. Not wanting to be surrounded on all sides by strangers, Katherine turned abruptly to see who was coming while managing to almost keep her back out of Mr. LaCroix's reach. When she didn't move fast enough, the person behind her, Ethan, grabbed her by the shoulders and shuffled her to the side.

Katherine huffed but she didn't have time to say one word before Ethan said to the lord of the were-peacocks, "Is there a problem, Mr. LaCroix?"

"Not that I know of," murmured the still-naked Thomas. Katherine wasn't peeking. Honest. But that much skin was hard to miss.

"Perhaps the lord of the were-peacocks would like to put on some clothes, then?" said Ethan with raised eyebrows and a chilly tone.

Before Mr. LaCroix could say his answer, the queen's voice rang out, "I insist. Stop this silliness, Thomas. We have much to discuss and much more to act upon."

"And a short time to do it," the fire marshal said while holding his hat in his hands anxiously. He wasn't nervous about LaCroix, Katherine noted, he was nervous around her mother. It had been that way all her life. When the queen entered the room time seemed to stop and everyone wanted to please her—non-family, that is. She was beloved in the community, so much so that Katherine would have suspected her blood was laced with aphrodisiacs if she hadn't been from the same bloodline. No one loved Katherine the way they adored her mother, though. Not that she wanted to. As the focus of the fire marshal, the were-peacock lord, and even Ethan shifted to the queen Katherine could see just how creepy it was. But her mother took it as her due.

She spread her hands out, sat, and said, "Shall we get on with why we're here?"

Mr. LaCroix lifted his hand and snapped imperious fingers. Out of the kitchen hurried a dainty woman with blonde hair, a short sky-jump nose, and a petite form. She hurried over to Mr. LaCroix's side as if summoned with a silk robe in her hands that her lord took from her quickly.

The now-clothed were-peacock pack leader turned to the queen with a flourish. "When my queen calls me, I come." He smiled and bowed.

"Do you know why I've called you?"

"In the dead of night?" said Thomas with purr. "I'd hope for something very entertaining."

The lasciviousness in his tone left Katherine squirming. That was her *mother*, for gosh sakes.

Her mother apparently didn't appreciate it, either. The Queen of Sandersville stood and slammed her hands onto the chestnut table.

"Let me put it to you simply, Lord LaCroix," she said. "My daughter is dead, a significant portion of my people have taken ill, and I believe that you are the cause. Why don't you tell me why I shouldn't have you beheaded this very minute?"

The man straightened uneasily at his queen's tone as he ran his now-shaky hands on the lapels of his robe as if to assure himself the cloth was still there. Katherine could feel tension blow through the room like an icy breeze.

Then she stiffened as she felt the temperature drop. *It's not metaphorical at all. It's physical.*

Katherine shifted her gaze to her immobile mother and wondered at how large the fury that was running through her must be for the queen's emotions to drop the temperature in the room without an outward sign—no flicker of her fingers, no murmur from her lips, just cold, hard emotional fury transforming her emotional distress into a tangible manifestation The longer the queen waited for an answer, the colder the room grew.

An audible gulp came from Mr. LaCroix's area. It could have been the servant girl. Katherine highly doubted it.

Then he spoke. "Your Highness, I assure you, one monarch to another, neither I nor my people have had nothing to do with any *illnesses* in the coven community."

A brittle smile appeared on her mother's face. "As we stand on ceremony, I expect you to address me as Your Majesty, Provincial Queen of Sandersville. As *your* superior, that respect is due to me."

A tic appeared at the corner of Mr. LaCroix mouth's as he listened to the queen's words, but he was too well bred...or too afraid...to state his objections.

Satisfied, Katherine thought, *As well he should be afraid. He stands before his provincial queen as proud as a peacock on game day. But he, and we, all know the respect due to a witch queen from her fae underlings, up to and including the lords and monarchs who represent each community.*

Mr. LaCroix, apparently realizing the precarious position he inhabited, swiftly bowed deep at the waist to his queen, even going as far as to bow so deeply that the posture was almost submissive in nature rather than simply the bow deemed necessary from a high-ranking lord second in rank only to his provincial queen.

Katherine watched as he didn't move and held the position, waiting for the queen's command to rise.

In short order her mother gave it.

"Rise," she said, sounding contemplative.

The man stayed where he was. "If I have offended Your glorious Majesty, a thousand apologies. From the rays of the mostly heavenly sun, I will bring you a gift that will surpass all others for the oversight."

Well, he certainly knows how to smoothly talk himself out of a situation, Katherine thought.

"Your oversight is forgiven, Mr. LaCroix. Now rise!" the queen commanded in a tone that said her patience was being taxed.

When he did so, the queen let out a slow breath. "You're a smart individual. You know I would not call you here for any reason other than a dire threat to our community and the sanctity of the population, Mr. LaCroix."

"You have always put the well-being of your people first, my queen. A tribute to your kindness, generosity, and fair rule," he answered gamely.

"And yet, my people are suffering," the queen said icily as she took her seat.

"Suffering, Your Majesty?" Mr. LaCroix asked with a helpless look that would have been well placed on an orphan.

Katherine's mother was unmoved as she titled her head and said, "Yes. The faerie of Ceidian's court are ill, quite ill."

Mr. LaCroix opened his mouth to protest and the queen held up a forestalling hand. Katherine wasn't quite sure if he planned on saying he had no idea about their illness or deny general wrongdoing in any case, but it didn't matter. One didn't screw up one's face and make their mouth in an O in order to agree with a charge against themselves.

Katherine was beginning to wonder if her mother would ever accuse Mr. LaCroix of anything or if she intended it to be all sidestep and innuendo for the rest of the night. If she did, Katherine knew fairly well how this would end. A light slap on the wrist for the were-peacock lord. After all, her mother abhorred capital punishments in the form of the death penalty. He would get a hefty fine, which Mr. LaCroix, thanks to his shipments, could easily pay and be on his way.

She was in for a surprise with her mother's next words, however.

"I do not care for your protests. All of my evidence, carefully gathered before my daughter's death, leads to you and your shipments," said the queen.

"Your Majesty," protested Mr. LaCroix with an elegant sweep of his hand that almost had Katherine laughing into her fist. The man just managed to make a bathrobe look stately, but even he couldn't make the goop laden in his hair evaporate or look any more suave in bare feet.

"Every fortnight from three forty-five a.m. until four fifteen a.m. you receive shipments of rare moon nectar," the queen interrupted. "Moon nectar that I allowed you to bring in for one reason—to break the monopoly the faerie king had on the distribution of the product in Sandersville. I agreed to this in order to not only break down their network but also to give Ceidian a cause to fear. He relies far too much on the sale and trade of the substance and was growing too entrenched for his own good."

Katherine's respect for her mother's tenure as queen grew. She only saw the day-to-day monotony of her mother signing municipal orders in her office or meeting boring groups of farmers who came to argue about grain levies. This, this was underhanded. This was sneaky. It was almost *queenly*.

"Yes, Your Majesty," said Mr. LaCroix as he eased into the conversation smoothly. "And so I did as you commanded. I have broken his hold and handed you more in the meantime."

"As well as handed yourself an open market," the queen said softly while resting her chin on her peaked hands. "Because, you see, I ordered you to loosen up his stranglehold on distribution, not grab it all for yourself by making addicts of his buyers and sellers in addition to draining their powers."

An affronted look crossed the were-peacock's face. "I wanted nothing to do with their powers, just a better market share for myself."

As if that was the worst of the crimes the queen had lobbied at him.

Maybe it was, Katherine thought to herself. *What could be worse than stealing someone's power? The very essence of their being?*

"Unfortunately, you're a known liar. You protest your innocence prettily, but I must say that I don't believe you," said the queen with mocking sadness as she leaned back into the hard-backed panel of the chair.

Then, with a snap of her fingers, six of her guardians came into the room. Four surrounding Mr. LaCroix from far enough away that Katherine could still easily see Mr. LaCroix's face, one standing behind the queen's chair, and another putting a hand on Katherine's shoulder to pull her back toward the French doors and exit into the hall.

Katherine let him drag her back a few steps, but she refused to leave the room and shook off his tugging hand from her shoulder with an irritated jerk. This was just getting good. There was no way she was leaving now.

Shock poured over the were-peacock's face and the tiny woman beside him gasped as she tried to hide behind her lord.

The sound of the front door opening didn't startle the queen or her lord's eyes from each other. Cecily came to stand by Katherine, and to Katherine's dread, the queen's headman stepped around to the left of the lord of the were-peacocks. His axe at the ready in his hands.

Katherine's mother cocked her head to the side with an ice-cold look in her eyes. "You have sixty seconds to convince me otherwise, Lord LaCroix, and give me a reason to spare your life."

CHAPTER FIFTEEN

Mr. Thomas LaCroix turned as pale as Katherine had yet seen him. He looked like he might faint. But he rallied.

"And what, Your Majesty, would convince you to spare my life?" he said.

"An antidote," the queen said simply.

"There isn't one," he said while clutching the female servant close. He and the woman seemed to shrink into themselves with his statement. If he had been in were-form, Katherine was sure his proud display of spread feathers would have been plastered to his skin and the musky odor of fear an ever-present scent in the room. But there wasn't and the two individuals on trial weren't, so she had to look for visual clues on LaCroix's present body and for his skin form, by all appearances human, to figure what he was feeling, what he was planning, and what could possibly go wrong next.

So he does care for someone beside himself, Katherine thought. *Who knew it was possible?*

Then Katherine took a closer, more uncharitable look at his stance. He was holding the woman still in a position equidistant from the two guardians to the northeast and southeast of him. If Katherine didn't know any better, she would think he was using the woman as a *shield*, which wasn't a stupid idea. Evil and creepy, but not stupid. If he threw the servant at the closest guardian in an attempt to flee, that would make the were-peacock's escape that much easier.

Katherine's lips pressed together firmly, signaling her disapproval.

What is it they say about cowards? 'Better a fool's death than a waste of a coward's breath?' she thought to herself.

Until that moment she hadn't really known what the seemingly nonsensical statement meant. But she had to admit now that she knew. But seeing as this entire night seemed to be one mystery after the other, it seemed rather appropriate that a nonsensical statement fit a rather unconventional standoff. Even though she didn't quite get anything that was currently happening, there was one thing Katherine Thompson did know, however. She would rather see Mr. LaCroix quartered and hanged than free and fleeing.

The guardians apparently were thinking along the same lines, because with a signal from their leader standing at the northwest corner of the quadrant, all four lifted their hands and glowing red pikes appeared. That was the great thing about guardians. They could summon any weapon to their hands that they chose, magical or mundane. She had seen them call in everything from old-time swords to the guns they always kept holstered at their shoulders. This time they had chosen pikes, and it didn't take a neurosurgeon to figure out why.

At a nod from the queen, the guardians lowered their pikes until each rested in the air no more than a foot from the were-peacock's face on all sides. A male guardian spoke. "By orders of the Provincial Queen of Sandersville, I have orders to execute either of you if you so much as move more than a few centimeters."

Katherine expected her mother to countermand that order that sounded like it was based on a prior conversation. Perhaps plans put in place prior to the arrival of the were-peacock lord and his servant? But no, her mother didn't make a move to increase the comfort of the two figures who stood as almost one body in the center of the room. Instead she nodded, smiled, and said, "Why do we need to be so formal?"

The queen's tone was mocking and completely different from anything Katherine had previously heard echo from her mother's mouth.

It's almost chameleon-like how she changes from mother to queen from one second to the next, Katherine thought. She had to wonder if her mother even remembered that she was present or if she had assumed that Katherine had been removed from the room by a guardian.

Taking stock of her surroundings, Katherine acknowledged that even though she had the perfect view of the proceedings and the flustered were-peacock lord between the guardians, those same guardians at least partially blocked her from view of the queen's eyes.

Katherine's mother continued speaking unabated. This time her voice like ice as she leaned forward. "If you so much as attempt to change your skin form into your were form, I'll be forced to retroactively sign your death warrant, Mr. LaCroix, because you'll be dead long before you hit the skies, and I won't be the sorrier for it. Just one headache lighter for an already excruciating day."

The last sentence was the queen's only acknowledgement of the suffering she had already gone through today. Otherwise her face was calm, her expression was icy, and her entire demeanor radiated swift justice. She was the absolutely opposite of the frazzled and distraught woman Katherine had seen earlier today.

How does she do that? She wondered absentmindedly as she watched the action in the room as if were a play-by-play of the much-loved human and ogre sport of boxing. Katherine felt at once both an impartial observer and a participator in the central scandal. Up until her mother's abrupt twelfth-hour call, she had been in charge of getting the answers as to why the faerie community was sickened with a moon nectar addiction that not only caused them to waste away like husks in the wind but also stole their very power from their bodies. She felt responsible for those individuals in a way she never had before, and it made her slightly uneasy.

So she was both apprehensive that her mother's strong-arming tactics wouldn't work to get an answer and a cure and relieved that it was someone else's duty, the *queen's* duty instead of the heir's, to solve this horrendous small-town crime.

I guess I can't ever call life in Sandersville boring again, Katherine thought wryly as she ignored an itch in her eye that she firmly told herself she'd deal with later. She didn't want to draw attention to her presence in the room now. Besides, it was more than an itch. As long as she ignored the sensation it would wait and simmer, like an itch at the corner of her eye. That itch that represented more than a space of skin in need of being scratched, it was the patch on her mind and heart that was holding closed a dark well ready to burst open with the rush of emotions boarded up behind its cap.

No matter how it felt to hold back the well of frustration and sadness, she had to. Katherine knew that in the same sense that she knew that, after today her life would never be the same again. So she held back her emotions of rage, pain, fear, and horror. Because right now was the time to attend to her duties, however and whatever form they appeared in. After that...after Mr. LaCroix was met with justice, after the dark faerie emerged from their drugged haze and were on the road to recovery, after she and Cecily found out what happened, and after Rose was laid to rest...when she had her answers, then they would come. But right now she didn't have the time or the energy for a cry-fest. What she wanted and what she needed was *answers.*

"We can't fly," squeaked the female servant. Perhaps an attempt to relay how non-dangerous they were or just a statement blurted out in sheer panic.

Nevertheless, the queen responded, "Perhaps not very far, but even a few feet is too much in my opinion."

The lord of the were-peacocks didn't deign to acknowledge either the queen or the lead guardian's statement, but he did wipe the sweat from his brow and push the servant girl away from him in disgust.

"I told the truth, Queen Leanna," he pleaded. "There is no antidote to give. But I have something better."

The queen leaned back with suspicious eyes. "And what would that be?"

Mr. LaCroix smiled with a crafty look that made Katherine want to wipe the smirk off his face herself. If that was too gauche for her Southern-born and bred mother, then Katherine wasn't above ordering the guardians to do it for her with a swift one-two punch to the smirking were-peacock's stomach.

The idea surprised her…not because of the spiteful feelings that welled up inside her, but because the idea of punishing him for his pride even amidst his downfall was one she was comfortable with. Hell, more than comfortable with. The man stood there, a threat to all they stood for—the protection of the people and the town they called home. Katherine realized she would do a lot more than order him punched to protect their residents.

She may not have wanted to inherit this small, piece-of-shit town in the middle of nowhere, but now that it was *hers,* or going to become hers, she was startling to feel some responsibility for it. Responsibility and righteous anger towards anyone who threatened it.

Katherine turned to get a better view of her mother as she thought, *perhaps we're not so different after all.*

Her mother's threats, her taunts, and her superior positioning over the were-peacock lord all served a purpose: to protect her people. If she had to do that with a cold demeanor, feudal tactics, and threats, then so be it. She was a *queen*, and queens ruled.

Finally, her mother stood up.

Fear swept over the man's face. Blatant fear.

Katherine watched with cautious calm. Wondering what would happen. What would her mother do to force this sniveling weasel to give up his knowledge? To give up what he knew for the betterment of all?

If she had expected her mother to go soft at the last minute, she would have been dead wrong. Good thing she hadn't.

Katherine knew her mother was a Southern belle. Proud of her heritage, careful of her looks, endlessly obsessed with community gossip, and not above letting a nice-looking warlock open a door for her.

Hell, Katherine thought with a grin, *Dad died. She didn't. Why shouldn't she appreciate the finer points of a male figure and a gentlemen?*

But Katherine also knew her mother had a backbone of steel. If a disagreement, never a fight, erupted between her and her girls…she never backed down. But she knew how to sugarcoat her firm hand with sweet compliments. There was no way else Katherine would have gotten up before dawn for the last six years to escort Gestap out if her mother had been anything but inflexible, determined, and so sweet about it that it was hard to say no.

Then a door opened with a loud creak that had everyone on edge. Not the door that led to this room, but the entrance to the house. The guardians were a little edgier than others. Two of them whipped out guns, one had a long knife in his hands, and other three kept their pikes.

"Weapon for everyone," whispered Katherine a tad hysterically. They'd never been on edge like this before. But the death of an heir and the capture of were-lord would put anybody on their toes, she guessed.

Katherine had to wonder where the outside guardians were and why they hadn't warned their compatriots, but they weren't in the dark for long. One of the guardians went to the French doors and passed through at the wave of hand from another guardian, who Katherine now was sixty-five percent sure was the captain. To her surprise, it was Cecily he came back with, firmly leading her by the shoulder with a stiff hand.

Cecily looked a little grim, which was understandable given the day and night they were having. But when she came into the room and saw the situation, she turned downright pale.

"Niece," said the queen sharply. "What brings you here? I instructed your guardian to take you home. To my sister's home."

Cecily stopped staring at the Mr. LaCroix and barely caught Katherine's eye before she turned her full attention on her aunt, hastily curtsying in a graceful manner that Katherine had never quite managed—especially under pressure—and said, "Forgive me, my queen. But I had urgent news for Katherine about a situation from earlier tonight. I was told she'd be here."

The queen nodded. "Would that situation be the addiction and power vacuum within the dark faerie court?"

"It would, my queen."

"Would this information be vital to my judgment of the were-peacock lord, Mr. Thomas LaCroix?"

Cecily hesitated. "I believe it would, my queen. Very much so."

"This is outrageous," Mr. LaCroix complained before Cecily could get a further word in.

The queen turned a sharp eye on him. "If I hear so much as a word leave from your mouth while the girl speaks, I will have it sewn shut for a week."

Mr. LaCroix snapped his mouth closed with an audible *click* of his teeth and bowed his head. To her mother, it would probably look like deference. To Katherine it looked like a way to hide the desperation in his gaze. She wondered how desperate he would be before the night was over.

"Then step forward, child," the queen said solemnly, "And tell all those present. Do not fear. No more of my blood shall perish today. Not if I have any say in the matter."

"Yes, yes, my queen," Cecily stammered nervously as she stared at Katherine's mother. She'd likely never seen her like this before. That was all right. Neither had Katherine.

CHAPTER SIXTEEN

With a beckon of the queen's impatient hand, Cecily sidled forward until she stood in the center of the room but far enough away from Mr. LaCroix that he couldn't graze her with the slightest touch of his body. Not that he'd want to, as she was standing almost between the guardians on his perimeter and they were likely to cut off the tips of his fingers for the infraction.

Then Cecily spoke. "I did as close to a substance bio-analysis as I could manage with only coven-available skills."

The queen raised her eyebrows in an unspoken question.

Cecily responded without pause, "The herbalist, Marsha, was able to preside over the study. When we were sure of what we had found, I came straight here."

The queen nodded.

Cecily continued as she handed over a small vial of glowing white liquid, "As I was saying, this substance was used to intoxicate the faerie people. At its core, it is the same moon nectar imbibed recreationally by the faerie people, which is non-lethal."

Katherine listened to Cecily intently. She was nervous at first, but the more she spoke the more confident she grew—in demeanor and tone.

Her cousin continued, "But a new variant was introduced to that core. A variant that, when added in crystallized form to the moon nectar, not only gives the faerie that ecstasy-like connection to the other realm that they so desperately seek…"

That was news to Katherine. The other realm had been closed off to any earthbound fae who resided on this side of the Atlantic Ocean for centuries. A mystical world that paralleled their own with one key difference, it was almost more myth than reality for their people now since many couldn't make the journey to cross the border. The faerie most of all. When they became settlers in the New World, they gave up many of their tributes from the Old One—access to the other realm being one of the most controversial.

But the high queens of the old European courts had been adamant. They wouldn't have rival queens setting up empires in new, virgin territories. These ship-bound queens would settle the land for them and rule in their stead, but they would *not* affect the magical covenants between fae, human, and coven. So those old queens had continued on doing what they did best. Interfered. They weaved a joint spell so powerful that those queens couldn't access the rift between this world and the next one. And if those queens couldn't do so, then none of their subjects could either. Creatures like the dark faerie, a people who originated from the other realm, had signed up for the voyage across the seas for a sense of daring and adventure. But they knew they would only stay in the New World for a year. Two at most. They had to return home, where their old queens could open the rift and allow them access to what their heart desired above all other things: the other realm.

They would only stay in the colonial lands for so long because of that. And so the most powerful fae subjects of the new coven queens cycled in and out of their territories. Never letting them become confident in their seats before a new wave came in, new negotiations began, and the young, stalwart queens had no choice but to accept this as fact.

The high queens of Europe had thought that the matter was settled then. They had confidently stuffed young, nubile queens on boats for the New World and instructed them to report back with their findings as well as to procure wealth for their titular queens' courts. But something changed along the way. Some sense of independence grew.

Well, the last laugh had been on those old queens. The new blood queens had not only affected those covenants but *broken* them in their revolutions for recognition as high queens' who were equal in power to their sisters across the ocean.

Broken them enough to give the queens of the new land independence. Even power. From the stories told of her ancestors' great, if not necessarily heroic, deeds, Katherine had learned that they had made a covenant between the thirteen original high queens of the Atlantic. A covenant that had repercussions to this day. But one that stabilized the land and stopped the endless cycle of fae returnees—the key to a thriving magical and mystical community.

But nothing could break the old queens' spell and allow the colonial queens what they wanted most: access to the *rift*. So when Cecily said this new strain of the moon nectar gave all of the dark faerie a sense of access to what was for them *a homeland*, she suddenly understood the appeal. What would cause dozens of the fairie, who weren't stupid, to imbibe the substance. They had what centuries of their colonial brethren had been unable to obtain, a connection to home, no matter how slight of a connection—it mattered.

Because a queen who couldn't give her subject what they sought most risked losing them entirely. The only reason war hadn't erupted sooner was because the old queens had vengefully, and some said sadistically, put an armed blockade along the sea wall that extended from the moors of Scotland to the inlets of the Carthaginian Empire. There was no way for the blood descendants of the original fae adventurers to return home to the land that would allow them access to the other realm even if they wanted to.

Cecily said, "A connection like that would be powerful. An aphrodisiac in itself and I can estimate is the reason why they would risk so much. In fact, they're taking the drug so much that they're overwhelming their own sense of self-preservation."

"How so?" murmured the queen in a fascinated manner, with rapt attention on Cecily. There wasn't an eye turned away from Cecily, except for Mr. Thomas LaCroix. Katherine's gaze sharpened on him as he dipped his head and bowed his shoulders, almost as if in resignation.

If Katherine had doubted her cousin's words a moment before, she didn't now. Mr. LaCroix knew it as the truth, she could tell from his demeanor…and the aura of muted anger that surrounded him like a red, hazy glow. But soon the whole room would know the truth, the full of it. Not just bits and pieces.

"They have to consciously lower the shields between their magical cores and the outside world," Cecily said almost reluctantly as the room gasped in astonishment.

That was tantamount to saying the faerie had agreed to assisted suicide. The faerie people were one of the few fae peoples that gained access to magic internally from birth. They didn't have learn it. They didn't call it. They didn't practice it. It was just there, like an extra part of their being that responded to their every living will. But their internal source had one major fault. It was finite and they couldn't gather more of their power or their magic from nature or the elements like a witch or many other fae could. The source, in fact, was incapable of being replenished outside of the other realm. This was, in part, why the faerie kings and queens were subjected to the rule of the coven queens on both sides of the Atlantic. In the old world, the coven queens had controlled access to the other realm. Enforcing concordant after concordant along the way with their sister queens and brother kings of the faerie. But the colonial coven queens had no such access to another realm and the faerie were forced to age and wither away bit by bit, like the humans and coven did. Without access to the endless fountain of power from their homeland, they were no longer immortal. In fact, they were *vulnerable*.

Vulnerable to death. Vulnerable to pestilence. Vulnerable to addiction.

But none were more vulnerable than when they let their shields down.

"Why would they do such a thing?" Katherine asked in amazement.

A voice answered from closer to the doors, "Power."

Katherine turned to see the owner of the voice even though she knew who had spoken before her eyes confirmed her thoughts. She'd actually forgotten he was in the room.

"Power to be as they once were," said Ethan with dark finality. He stopped then. Hesitant to move forward into the room, a room where a queen, an heir, her blood, and her guardians reigned. Even an ally would step carefully on such grounds. Katherine's mother was a fair ruler, but what was fair and what was right in the heat of the moment could be tricky, and Ethan probably didn't want to step in unwanted.

But Queen Leanna turned to him with a look that encouraged him to continue speaking without words.

"I've been living among the faerie court for months," Ethan said with a deep swallow. "When they took the enhanced moon nectar they knew what they were doing. If anything, only Ceidian was kept in the dark. At first, they lost little by little only what they thought they could regain tenfold if they could harness the drug to force a connection to the other realm."

"Only the queens of Europe can do that," Katherine whispered, almost as if to deny it.

Ethan shrugged. "It's been centuries since any of them had tasted their homeland. Centuries since they had hope. Some of the people you saw tonight are second-generation colonials, even *third*. As each generation came into existence, they saw their natural powers weaken and knew there would come a time when their children would be nothing but whispers of what a true faerie of the old courts would be. Their internal cores were dwindling no matter what they did. And less-powerful parents produce less-powerful offspring. You know that."

Ethan paused and glanced at Katherine. It was an awkward look.

Katherine grimaced. It was unspoken rule that less-powerful coven queens were born from low-blood matriarchy. It was why provincial queens almost always had nurturing powers, like the ability to call upon the winds and rain for a bountiful harvest or an emotional gift to calm the masses. It was the high queens of the thirteen provinces who had the true gifts. Gifts only whispered about, gifts that Katherine could only shiver thinking about. A shiver of fear...and anticipation. She wouldn't be a red-blooded teenager if she didn't want to see at least one high queen in action in her lifetime. Most of her teenage witch and warlock classmates could talk of nothing else but a homecoming trip to Atlanta, to attend the High Queen of Georgia's night festival, and see her in life as well as taste the magic of her gift, which was said to shiver in the air like a living wind.

Katherine would be a fool if she said she wasn't looking forward to the same excursion two years from now, during her senior year. The idea always brought an excited thrill running through her, but now...now she felt a little apprehensive. Until tonight, she hadn't been able to imagine why seniors given a taste of that high queen's magic and her court would ever want to return to Sandersville or the surrounding provincial counties. But return they did. Year after year, even though they were given a queen's gift upon high school graduation. One gift, and it was choice—one year of sponsorship in the lower courts of the Atlanta high queen or one year of apprenticeship with a local coven member to learn a trade. Without fail, every single graduating member of the coven high school class, all thirty of them on average, had chosen the apprenticeship.

With the dark taste of her mother's gaze, as intoxicating and deadly as staring into a serpent's small eyes, Katherine knew why they wouldn't want to go back for a year now. Rumors of the darkness of the high queen's court aside, if a provincial queen could summon such nefarious magic, how much stronger and more terrifying would a high queen's gifts be?

Katherine shivered, then Ethan broke eye contact with her, and she shook her head to clear her thoughts of reverie.

"They felt they had no choice," Ethan said in misery. "The faerie people know they are dying out. Even if Ceidian won't admit it...*can't* admit it to himself."

"So they took action," concluded the queen.

"So they took action," Ethan said quietly.

Katherine's face twitched in denial. But the heavy darkness in the room, the horror of the truth that echoed in Cecily and Ethan's words, and the silence of the were-peacock lord told everyone all they needed to know. They knew in their hearts, even if their minds couldn't comprehend a connection so strong that an individual would slowly allow their life to be drained away to access it again.

Katherine blinked and said aloud before she could think about it. "But what about their *power*? It had to go somewhere. Lowering their shield's made them vulnerable, but it's not like their gifts leaked out on their own."

"Katherine is right," Cecily said with a shudder. "They were siphoned away."

"Can they be siphoned back?" the queen asked.

Cecily shook her head. "From what I was able to determine, my queen, I think not. What's done is done."

The queen knelt down to peer into the eyes of the were-peacock lord. "What say you, Thomas? Is my niece right?"

The man shuddered as the queen's forefinger lifted his lowered chin inch-by-inch.

"What's done is done?" she continued coldly.

He turned defiant eyes up to his queen. "The girl is right."

The queen smiled. A bitter one. "Tell me, Thomas. What were you doing with all of these gifts? What could be so necessary that you would break the sacrosanct agreements between the fae communities to do this?"

For the first time that evening the man laughed, and it was dark and rich. Almost evil.

"Money," he whispered. "It's always money."

The queen dropped her finger from his chin as she leaned back in disgust.

"I sold every drop of power to the highest bidder in five counties," he said with a nervous lick of his lips. "There's nothing left on me."

"And no way to reverse it," Cecily said.

"What about the addiction?" the queen asked.

"I don't know," Cecily answered truthfully.

By the time she was finished, her voice was firm with only the hint of a tremor. Then the queen nodded and turned her head away to think.

That's my girl, thought Katherine, proud of her cousin's strong demeanor.

As Katherine turned a troubled gaze back on her mother, who now stood facing forward, she wasn't sure what to expect. Sick horror. Pained understanding. What she hoped to see was firm resolution and a queen ready for decisive action no matter how distasteful the punishment would be.

She got that and more. Her mother's face was blank. Instead of steel with a sweet nature shining forth, Katherine saw her eyes hardened in anger. Then she realized something important.

Sweet steel was her mother's persona as a homemaker.

Finely honed calculation was her persona as a *queen*.

"One last chance," purred the queen.

The man stiffened his spine. "I have nothing left to give."

"You mean you're not willing to give it," replied the provincial queen.

A tic appeared at the corner of the man's mouth.

Irritation, perhaps? Katherine wondered as she studied his face. *Or perhaps a sign that Mother's interrogation is getting to him?*

Fear was fine. But fear didn't make every man break. No, sometimes it was the stupid things. Like pride. Like the need to be superior. Perhaps it would be that chauvinist pride that would cause this were-peacock lord's downfall.

The queen's eyes narrowed. "Oh, yes. I know, Thomas. I've known since we walked into this room. A large amount still resides in you. Because the faerie power cannot live outside a host for very long. An hour at most. You might have sold a portion, but you, you are filled with a flaring magic that emits light like a honing beacons inside you. *You* still have their gifts."

CHAPTER SEVENTEEN

Naked fear appeared on his face. Katherine sucked in a surprised breath. *He's bluffing.*

"But that's all right," the queen said gaily. "Because I'm sure you've discovered that harvesting and *using* those gifts are two very, very different things."

The man licked dry lips.

Katherine narrowed her eyes.

"Oh, yes," the queen said with a brittle smile. "Which is why you've been selling it off bit-by-bit, haven't you? Can't use it yourself, not as a fae of the Earth. Only one of the shining could rip the power from another for personal purposes. Now the question is...how to get it out of you?"

Mr. LaCroix swallowed. "I can share it...with whomever you want. Name a person."

"But then the gift becomes theirs," Ethan blurted out in interruption. "Give the power to another living being and it cannot be returned to the fae host. It has to be an inanimate carrier. At least for a short time."

The queen nodded. "I know."

Mr. LaCroix sat back on his heels. Sullen. "Fine, whatever carrier you choose."

"Yes," purred the queen. "But first your punishment."

The man looked up at with a snarl. "What is your will, my queen?"

He knew now that he wouldn't be killed. Because the queen still needed him for the transfer. So whatever she decided to punish him with—a public sentence, a length of time in the human slammer—would be nothing he couldn't deal with.

He knew it and they knew it. Katherine could almost see the confidence regrouping in his eyes.

The queen tilted her head. "My will is a punishment that fits the crime."

A small exhale of breath escaped Katherine's mouth as her eyes grew wide.

The queen continued, "For the crime of attempted murder, Mr. Thomas LaCroix will bear the same action."

The were-peacock lord's head flew back in genuine surprise. Katherine wasn't quite sure what her mother was decreeing, but he certainly knew.

The queen looked over at a guardian out of the corner of her eye. "Bring the lash."

That startled a laugh out of the man. "You can't be serious," he said.

"Oh, I am," the queen replied.

As the guardian quickly returned with an ebony whip made of leather that shined with oil, Katherine felt a shiver run down her spine. The lash was as thick as a snake's tail and as dark as a black mamba's scales. Equally deadly with a fatal bite, Katherine felt cold as she watched the snake-like whip uncoil in her mother's hands.

Cecily outright shrank back from the loose whip's coils. It lay like a placid snake at Katherine's mother's feet before it would sing through the air with a sharp whistle as it struck.

The queen glanced coolly at her niece.

"Cecily, dear," said the queen, "I think it's time that you left."

Cecily whimpered even as she said, "I'd rather stay."

With open fear on her face, Katherine wondered why she'd push the issue. But it didn't matter.

"I'd rather you not," the queen said in a tone like ice a few seconds later. She flicked a finger at a guard who firmly grabbed Cecily by the arm and escorted her out the door.

Katherine steeled her spine, expecting to be next with Ethan. She balled angry fists and crossed her arms hastily in order to avoid looking like a petulant child banished from the playground. She didn't think she succeeded.

But the movement certainly caught her mother's attention.

The queen's quick glance at her only living daughter's face was an assessment, a calculation, and a decision all rolled in one.

"Katherine, you will stay. You must witness the work of the queen. Because the heavens above and the hell below know that you will someday have to make such decisions yourself."

The queen's voice was final.

Katherine had to wonder, *who was this woman and were had the female that Katherine knew as Leanna Thompson gone?*

"Before I begin," Katherine's mother said gravely, "Thomas LaCroix, you are hereby sentenced to sixty lashes by your provincial queen's hand. For the crime of narcotics production and tampering as well as attempted murder. Do you recognize your crimes?"

Katherine let out an audible gasp. That was a death sentence. Were-creature or not.

The man gained some backbone...from somewhere...and stood with his back straight and his head held up proudly. He looked over the queen's head at the far wall, seeing nothing but acknowledging her words.

"I do," he answered.

"If given the option of forty-five lashes, will you willfully and without malicious intent, hand over the remainder of the faerie people's siphoned power?"

No expression changed on his peaceful face as he answered, "I would."

"And would this gift of power be enough to at least close the wounds in the faerie psyche?"

LaCroix grimaced but nodded. "With careful attention it can plaster over the opening they have made, but it's up to them not to open the wound again."

"Once they realize the depth of their mistake upon rising from the addictive haze," interjected Ethan. "I think Ceidian will be able to convince them of the merit of staying away from the tainted moon nectar."

LaCroix gave a bitter and mocking laugh. "Always the most hopeful, the young."

The queen hissed, "Not hope, LaCroix. Fear. Because Ceidian has one chance to get his people turned around. If he does not, he will deal with me."

The were-peacock lord silenced himself with effort then shrugged. "As you will it, my queen."

The queen nodded and cracked the whip. To the guardian standing beside her she said, "Bring the object."

The man rushed from the room and returned with an orb.

Without any further delay, the queen waved her hand and motioned the guard forward. With a wary look, the guardian stretched out his hand so that the orb glowed with a milky iridescent inches from Thomas LaCroix's face. With a grimace, LaCroix raised cautious hands and placed them on the orb. He closed his eyes, sighed deeply, and transferred the essence of the faerie gift from within him into the depths of the orb.

Katherine could *see* the transference. It was as if starlight flowed from LaCroix's heart, up his arms, and into the orb's glass exterior in a stream of bright light. Furiously blinding one moment and gone the next.

With a word, the guardian lowered his arm with the heavy-looking orb in his grasp and turned to his queen.

With a flick of her eyes, the queen looked over to Ethan. "Ethan Nestor, go with my guardian. Return the orb to the people who have given you a home, relay my sympathies to Ceidian, and ask him for a sit-down meeting with me in three days hence."

Ethan nodded, bowed to his queen, and left the room with the guardian carrying the prize in a stiff hand by his side. Katherine's mother followed her guardian's path with watchful eyes. Once he returned with a stiff nod, she turned back to LaCroix with a pleased smile.

"Well done," the queen said, pleased.

LaCroix said nothing. Instead he straightened his shoulders and dropped the silk robe that covered him from head to toe. He turned around so that his back faced the queen and his hands were outspread, solemn, contemplative.

The Queen of Sandersville sighed. In acceptance, in appreciation? Katherine didn't know.

Her mother's hand tightened on the whip as she lifted the limp black weight in her hand by the handle. Katherine knew she was standing much too close to the male to inflict damage with such a long whip. But still, two guardians stepped forward from the southwest and southeast corners of the group of four guardians watching over him.

One grabbed LaCroix's right arm. One grabbed LaCroix's left arm.

They held him tightly, waiting for their queen's orders. LaCroix bowed his head and awaited his punishment.

Leanna Thompson took two steps back in her long dark gown and raised her hand. As she did Katherine couldn't stop the whisper of surprise from escaping from between her lips. LaCroix turned his head slightly to the right to take a look at Katherine's face. The open surprise that must have been on her face obviously startled him, because he opened his mouth to speak.

By then it was too late.

Queen Leanna Thompson, Provincial Queen of Sandersville, Georgia of the original thirteen colonies of the New World, had transmuted the black coils in a saber made of an onyx. And that's when Katherine remembered why the sight of the onyx whip's coils had struck fear in her heart from the beginning. Nine years ago, on the anniversary of her father's death, the High Queen of Atlanta had paid an unannounced visit to the Queen of Sandersville's home.

She was the regnant queen of the entire province of Georgia, so she could go where she pleased. She had chosen to attend the remembrance ceremony for Katherine's father for one reason only—family obligation.

Yes, the High Queen of Atlanta was Katherine Thompson's great aunt. Although she had never once seen her before and had not seen her since. "Close" wasn't a word one would use to describe her relationship with Great Aunt Lysa. But she did honor the traditions, and coven ritual stipulated that all eligible blood relatives must attend the wake or the remembrance ceremony for any individual in the family who died. For some reason or another, Great Aunt Lysa had not been present for Katherine's father's burial.

When she had arrived at his remembrance ceremony, the mourning gift she bore had been very special. A chimera weapon that could transform into four separate weapons depending on the owner's preference—a long black whip, an onyx saber, reinforced knuckles made of black silver, and midnight throwing stars. All deadly weapons that were not out of place in a high court, or so Katherine had heard, but completely useless in a small town like Sandersville.

So Katherine's mother had put the present away as soon as it was polite to do so and they had all forgotten about it. Until now.

Mr. LaCroix spoke aloud, his voice a little high. "What's going on?"

His muscles strained as he tried to jerk from of the grips of the guardians on either side. But neither budged. They had the strength of ten oxen when called upon.

Without pausing a moment, the queen spoke in a deadly voice, "For the crime of disrupting the peace between the fae communities and stripping your brethren of their powers, Thomas LaCroix, I sentence you to death."

LaCroix's eyes bulged out in horror just as Katherine's left-handed mother swept back the saber and sliced straight through the were-peacock's neck. And that was the end of Mr. Thomas LaCroix.

Katherine Thompson watched in a daze as the seconds after his head left his body felt like an eternity. The arc of blood in the air. The surprise in his wide-open eyes. The flailing of lifeless arms up in the air. The fall of his body forward with a *thud* to the ground. It was a clean decapitation, as far as decapitations went. As LaCroix's head rolled across their hardwood floor, the blood from his severed neck sprayed in ever-widening circles. Katherine watched the head slowly roll until it came to a stop at the base of the china cabinet and blood began to pool on the floor from the body's emptying veins.

For the first time that night, Katherine got a sense of the magnitude in which her mother worked. And without batting an eye, she could easily say that she hadn't seen a tenth of who her mother really was. Not until now. Not until tonight.

Amazing how seeing your mother order someone decapitated brings all those prideful feelings to light, Katherine thought.

She was also feeling a bit smug at their similar mindset. For her entire life, it seemed, the queen and Rose were as tight as best friends, alike in so many ways, and different from Katherine in most others. But here...here was Katherine in her mother. Her streak of ruthlessness. Rose would have been far too squeamish to have the execution done. While Katherine stood with no little pride as blood dripped down the side of her face.

Looking up, her mother's eyes caught her own and Katherine watched the emotions play across the queen's face. Shock then cautious acceptance. The queen could see the smile on Katherine's face. She might not know what it meant, but she knew that her daughter approved of her choice of punishment.

She barely heard her mother order the guardians to remove the screaming servant girl and take the body outside for Gestap's early morning breakfast. "I believe my daughter will be too tired to feed him otherwise and put the head on a spike in the town center," the queen said before Katherine saw her mother walk forward to stand directly in front of her.

They stood so close together that the queen's dress spilled over onto Katherine's army boots.

Blinking rapidly, Katherine allowed her mother to tilt her face up and she listened with her heart frantically beating in her ears as the queen said, "We never negotiate with anarchists."

Then the queen dropped her finger from Katherine's chin and enfolded her only living daughter in her embrace. All Katherine could do was stand and watch the spilled red blood on the hardwood floor absorb into the dark wood as if had never existed.

Another of her mother's homemaker witch tricks, she was sure.

CHAPTER EIGHTTEEN

After a few seconds had passed, it was if a spell had broken and they were once more aware of each other and the room they stood alone in except for the heavy stench of fear and anger.

With a long sigh, the queen stepped back from the tight hug she had Katherine shared and trailed her hands up her daughter's long arms until both of her hands rested comfortably on Katherine's shoulders.

"This was an easier introduction to life at a court than I had," the queen said while massaging her daughter's shoulders as if she wanted to will away the tension in the room by easing the knots in Katherine's muscles.

Katherine choked back a dark laugh as she said, "Easier? What could be harder than watching an execution?"

Her mother's eyes caught her own in a searching manner.

"Watching an execution," her mother answered in a forthright manner. She wasn't making light of the situation; Katherine could tell she was just being honest.

Katherine shook her head in disbelief. Not quite believing her mother. The woman who baked her cookies every year for back-to-school, the woman who laughed at the local banker's horrible jokes and judged pig racing in the spring fields. Where had that woman gone, and who was this woman who chopped off a person's head in one minute and destroyed the evidence the next?

Katherine's horror and confusion must have shown on her face, because the queen closed her eyes for a moment, and when she opened them it was as if a window to her soul had been laid bare.

Hesitant her mother said, "Despite how this might look...this wasn't easy for me, Katherine. The decision. The manner of execution. But I will be honest and say it is something I'm used to."

Katherine shook her head. "What are you talking about?"

The queen's massaging hands stilled and then they traveled lower until she gripped tightly the flesh just above her daughter's elbows. "I tried to shield you and Rose from this."

"From what?" Katherine asked in a mystified tone.

"Death. Pain. Cruelty," her mother said. "Life at court, essentially."

Still Katherine didn't understand. "But this isn't court. This isn't who we are or who *you* are."

The queen smiled and leaned her forehead against her daughter's for just a moment before she stood straight again. "Oh, my daughter, that is exactly what I wanted you to believe growing up. To believe that court is the opposite of death, that it is life. To know that pain isn't the center of court, pleasure is. To abhor cruelty in any form, and to give kindness instead. And I succeeded all too well."

"But…" interrupted Katherine.

"No," her mother interjected. "Just listen."

Katherine stilled and then she nodded. It was a command, not a request.

"I raised you and your sister in the opposite manner I was raised," her mother said after taking a long breath. "I raised you to respect all communities, honor your duties even when it is the last thing you wish to do…"

Katherine flashed back on her reluctance earlier that day to have anything to do with the trolls' ceremony. It was true, she *hadn't* wanted to go. But she went.

"…and to think like a benevolent queen would and should. Even though I had no such role model myself," her mother finished. "But the truth of the matter is that most queens are cruel tyrants. In sheltering you and your sister and raising you in a community like this, I believe I stunted you in more ways than one. Ways that the humans would refer to as 'street smarts' in simplistic terms. Because my sister queens outside this small haven of Sandersville rule over their people in a quite different manner then I tend to do myself. They rule by power, blood, and force. Just like the court that I grew up in. The court that was once your grandmother's."

Her mother paused for a moment and Katherine took a moment to interject.

"But who was she? You've never told Rose and me about her, or any of our family, really. Not on your side of the family tree. We've never even *met* her," Katherine finished in a mumble.

"And you never will," her mother answered. "My mother is long gone from my life and so is my aunt. All that is left is your aunt, Cecily, and memories. It will stay that way."

Katherine wanted to protest, but the look in her mother's eyes said this wasn't the time. There was a time to be willful and a time to be obedient. The ten minutes after her mother had finished decapitating a man was definitely a time to be obedient.

Katherine asked a question tentatively, though. "So your life was different before you had us?"

"Much different," the queen affirmed with a slow nod of her head and a rueful look. "But now I feel that perhaps I have sheltered you girls too much. You must be able to stand on your own two feet."

"I can," declared Katherine defiantly.

Her mother raised an arched eyebrow, which was oddly distracting, as a streak of blood was drying just below her eye.

"You must be able to rule with a steady head *and* a courageous heart," her mother continued.

Katherine stiffened her shoulders and raised her hands to squeeze her mother's hands, which still rested on her upper arms. "I will."

The queen nodded thoughtfully. "And you must be able to kill without regret."

Katherine hesitated. "I can try."

Her mother shook her head. "There is no try, Katherine. At the high courts, and, I'm beginning to see, here as well, there is kill or be killed."

185

"That's a bit melodramatic, Mother," Katherine pointed out. "One deviant doesn't make an entire community deviant."

Queen Leanna smiled with a twitch of her lips that didn't reach her eyes. "More of the philosophy I taught you, I see. The issue is not with one deviant, but with what simmers underneath the surface. I know that Mr. LaCroix was only the tip of the iceberg in terms of the problems spreading across the countryside. He was a minor problem. We have more important people to deal with."

"Like who?" Katherine asked.

Her mother hesitated. For a moment it looked as if she would answer Katherine's question. Then she said, "Another time, Katherine. Another time. First you must not only learn how to defend your people, but also kill in their name. Because when I am gone, it will be left to you to protect Sandersville."

Katherine nodded. If felt like her world had turned upside down in less than twenty-four hours. Her sister—her only sister—had died and left a shitstorm for Katherine to clean up in her wake.

Katherine almost smiled. She wasn't delusional; she and Rose had *never* gotten along. It had been wishful thinking they could put aside their differences for more than a few minutes at a time, but Katherine did feel a responsibility to take up the mantle of her legacy. However slight. And shoulder the burden of ruling Sandersville alongside her mother.

And to think, she thought wryly, *this morning I was complaining about taking Gestap out to breakfast.*

Staring at her mother thoughtfully, Katherine said, "I understand now. But how do you learn to kill someone without regret? How do you go about it? Do you order others to do it or do it yourself?"

"It depends on the situation," her mother said with an elegant shrug. "But you will need to learn to kill with your own hands and your own magic."

Half of Katherine's mind was in a permanent state of disbelief that they were having this conversation at all. It was the most surreal moment in her life. When she had turned sixteen earlier this year, she had expected that she'd perhaps get 'the talk' about aligning herself with a powerful warlock, maybe get some lessons on dark blood rituals, and finally start to gain some independence and have some larks. She *hadn't* thought she'd been getting lessons on how to kill before she turned twenty-one.

Finally, after studying her face for a moment, her mother said, "And, Katherine?"

"Yes, Mother?" Katherine muttered, a little shell-shocked.

"It's also time you harnessed your gifts. *All* of them."

Katherine frowned and looked up. She hadn't missed the emphasis in her mother's voice. Did she know? Did she believe in the visions and the ghosts after all?"

The queen released her arms. "I don't know exactly what your blood gifts will bring to bear for you as a witch, but I know that your skill in contacting the elementals of the forest will come in handy. We'll start with that this week."

"Oh," Katherine said. Almost disappointed. She wasn't sure if she could handle more revelations or bonding with her mother tonight. But it would have been nice to understand something about *herself* tonight. Instead she'd learned her mother was a cold-blooded killing machine when called upon, the sleazy-but-now-dead were-peacock was a criminal mastermind, and a lot of the fae were dumber than they looked...the trolls included, which was a particularly hard thing to accomplish.

Still Katherine rallied her thoughts and nodded to her mother. "Very well."

"Good," said the queen, approval creeping into her voice.

As an involuntary shiver overcame Katherine's body, and her mother spied her skin shaking, she asked, "Are you all right, my darling?"

"I don't know," Katherine answered honestly.

"You will be," her mother said soothingly.

Katherine raised an eyebrow that her mother didn't see as she turned away to walk toward the French doors where Katherine was sure all of the guardians not assigned a task awaited her orders.

She guessed their conversation was over. But something itched in the back of her mind. Something that she wanted to voice, but couldn't.

Katherine wasn't entirely sure her *mother* was well.

"And where the hell is Aunt Sarah?" she whispered to herself as she followed the queen into the hallway.

Unlike the calm of the parlor they had stood in, the hallway and the entrance to the house was a clamor. A clamor mainly consisting of two people. The servant girl that Katherine had all but forgotten in the melee, a man Katherine recognized as the town funeral director who was pushing buttons on his little cell phone and stridently avoiding the grasp of a guardian hell-bent on taking the device away from him, and a rearing unicorn at the front door. Katherine did a double take at the last one, although they were all pretty weird.

She was more concerned that the unicorn's, *definitely* male, hooves were covered in its naturally dark orange blood.

"No offense to the unicorn," muttered Katherine to no one, "but he looks a right mess."

And he did. Because the orange blood was showing like neon paint against the unicorn's all-black fur. He looked like an extra prop in a Halloween house of fright. Add in the fangs that were just visible below the unicorn's trembling upper lip and the bright red eyes, and you had a legitimate unicorn from hell. Of course, he wasn't *actually* from Hell.

Nicern, was the leader of the local unicorn pack, and was what was considered a Licorn. At least that was the formal term for it. Katherine just normally referred to him and his kind as 'the blood-drinking unicorns from hell.' It was an apt title, as the entire unicorn pack were actually Licorns, since unicorns had all died out millennia ago from over-hunting, and they were all as bitchy as demons from the third tier of Lucifer's kingdom. Nicern being no exception. He could be mad about anything and drunker than a tick on a hellhound at all hours of the day. So Katherine's guess was as good as anyone's as to why he whinnying unintelligibly—after all, he *could* talk with only a slight lisp that no one dared point out due to the fangs.

Katherine tried plugging her ears against the inhuman whinnying, the very human-sounding screeches from the servant, and the outright yelling match between the guardian, who had succeeded in prying the phone away, and the funeral director, but it barely eased the jarring noise. And everyone but the two guardians at the door were too far gone into the madness to realize the queen had stepped into the room.

CHAPTER NINETEEN

Finally, Katherine lowered her hands to her mouth, inserted two fingers between her lips, and let out a screeching whistle so loud that it cut off the clamor instantly.

Her mother sighed with a grateful smile over her shoulder and said, "Thank you, Katherine."

The guardian, currently in a tug of war with the funeral director, straightened with a jerk of his arm, prying the cell phone that had been re-captured out of the lapsed funeral director's hand, and then Katherine recognized him as the leader of the queen's guardians.

"Your Majesty, if I may speak?" he said quietly.

"Proceed," the queen said regally while folding her hands at her waist.

Katherine's mother was studiously ignoring the fact that her gown was covered in blood and the guardian leader was stiffly at attention before his queen…also ignoring the obvious swath of red on his queen's gown.

Katherine rubbed her brow in irritation. *Am I the only one who sees that this is a really big deal?*

Looking around the hallway, Katherine had to admit that most of the guests looked half out of their minds, and the guardians…well, the guardians looked like they always did, passive and dour.

Then some hiccups, that were threatening to turn into a whimper, caught her attention. The only sound in the room was coming from the hunched over form that knelt on the ground, plastered as close to the wall as she could get and surrounded on two sides by guardians that were undoubtedly making her even more uncomfortable.

But it wasn't the guardians that the servant was staring at. It was the queen. Specifically the queen's bloodstained dress. As the servant's lower lip began to tremble, Katherine expected to see the waterworks flowing again. But, to her surprise, and probably the girl's, she held it together.

That is, until a new guardian came through the door that led to the house's kitchen carrying a pot, which he immediately turned on its side and presented to the queen and, by default, the entire room. The shrieks that erupted from the servant's mouth were enough to wake the dead.

Well, at least I'm not the only one upset, Katherine thought gratefully.

The queen grimaced at seeing Thomas's head in her cooking pot, but waved the guardian through. "Do as I commanded," she explained. "Straight to the town square and up on the headman's pike with a spell to keep it fresh for five days. The whole town will know my wrath for this one...*deviant.*"

Katherine didn't miss the fact that her mother used the word she had spoken to express her thoughts about LaCroix's actions.

Perhaps we can learn from each other, she mused. Well, her mother could teach her and Katherine could try to get her to see reason.

Eyeing the screeching servant girl, Katherine muttered, "Starting with her."

Firmly Katherine walked forward and knelt into front of the servant, effectively blocking her view of her mother and the retreating guardian. The were-peacock woman stared at Katherine with large eyes brimming with tears and trembling lips. She looked more like a girl than a woman at that moment, and Katherine had to wonder how old she was.

I've changed my mind, I don't want to know, she thought with a shudder as she remembered the servant coming forward to clothe her lord in a familiar manner, too familiar for one who wasn't intimate with his touch.

Calmly Katherine reached forward to grab the servant's hands, only pausing to give the guardian who reached out to stop her an irritated look. What was the girl going to do, claw her to death?

In any case, the servant let Katherine enfold her hands in her own and slowly pull her to her feet.

Trembling but standing, she faced Katherine with her head held high, which made the were-peacock's servant at least a foot taller than Katherine who was holding her up emotionally. But Katherine didn't mind. She was used to people towering over her, her mother and sister included. It didn't intimidate her anymore, even though it used to. And when you lived in a town with occasional giant caravans passing through, *everyone,* at some point in their lives, felt like the smallest person in the room.

"Deep breaths," Katherine counseled, easing into her own set of rhythmic deep breaths as she continued holding the woman's hands. Slowly the servant followed suit, as if mesmerized by Katherine's calm manner, and they synchronized their breathing.

Peacocks were vain, tedious, and flighty creatures in real life. And the weres that called them brethren didn't stray far from that personality tree. But they were also very much a communal species. Were-peacocks existed in large groups and rarely strayed far from each other. So Katherine could see how it would distress the woman to lose her leader and the only other were-peacock around for miles, or so Katherine assumed. She wasn't quite sure *where* her mother had ordered these two were-peacocks to be picked up from, but the were-peacock reservation was on the other side of the small town—that much she knew.

With her breaths even and her sobs abated, Katherine smiled at the servant and said, "Better?"

The woman nodded. "Th-thank you, mistress."

"No problem," murmured Katherine. "What's your name?"

The were-peacock glanced over nervously at the licorn who had stepped through the door, but she turned back to answer Katherine's query. "Nimestra."

"Well, Nimestra, what are you crying about?" Katherine asked softly.

The woman let out a breathy sigh. "He's dead. My master is dead."

"Yes, he is," her mother interrupted with finality. "But you are not. Bless your gods that you had none of the faerie power within you, and leave. Now."

The woman stood quivering, but she didn't make a move toward the door. Whether or not it was because Nicern's intimidating form was still standing in the door, Katherine would never know, because in the next moment the woman voiced a tremulous query.

"My queen?"

"Yes," answered Leanna from where she was already turned away to deal with the angry visitor on her front steps.

"I wish you to know," Nimestra said with an audible gulp. "None of the were-peacock community had any hand in Master LaCroix's plans. He…felt that we weren't worthy to carry it out."

"You mean he was a secretive bastard who didn't trust anyone but his own self," the queen offered not unkindly.

Nimestra blinked. "I…"

The queen waved a dismissive hand. "Never you mind; I know it is not done among your kind to speak ill of the dead."

Nimestra nodded gratefully. "Then I will take my leave as you command."

As Katherine watched Nimestra walk toward the door with a repressed look of anger at the guardians who had previously blocked her way, Katherine's mother called out, "Wait!"

Nimestra turned with a look of fearful surprise on her face. Much as her former master had looked numerous times in his last few minutes alive before the Queen of Sandersville.

The queen said, "Come here."

 194

Trembling Nimestra walked over to her and prepared to kneel.

A short 'no' from the queen stopped her. Then Katherine's mother gathered Nimestra's face between her hands. She didn't speak. She just looked deep into her eyes. Katherine's mother was standing an angle where she could see her face. There was no pity there. No regret. Only ice-cold desire.

Silently the queen dropped her hands away from Nimestra's face as Katherine saw tears begin to track down the poor, frightened woman's cheeks.

She thinks mother will execute her, too, Katherine thought silently. The trouble was, Katherine couldn't say with absolute certainty that she was wrong. But still, Nimestra was being braver than she had all night. She wasn't bawling, just silently crying. As the queen continued to stare unfazed, Nimestra hastily wiped her hands on her face. Perhaps to remove the dampness of the tears trailing down her cheeks. She only succeeded in smearing eye shadow and mascara along her cheeks with streaks of black and blue.

The woman didn't notice when she lowered her hands to her waist. To be fair, Katherine wouldn't have noticed, either. Not if she was trapped in a queen's gaze like the girl was. The gaze of a queen was different than the gaze of a witch. Her mother rarely used the technique, but Katherine could always feel her mother's witch presence build just before she tapped into the inherited rather than natural gift.

It was said to be like being mesmerized by the cold black eyes of a serpent in most cases. Katherine knew her mother could use the gaze to assess a person's intent and worth with a thought. But it was a frightfully dreadful look to be subjected to. Even standing to the side, Katherine felt gooseflesh rise on her arms as she watched the exchange of gazes.

Coldness swept into the room and Katherine knew it was due to her mother. Again. She began to wonder when this night would end, and the same time hoped it would continue. She had never seen so much of a queen's power and influence used in such a short time. Selfishly she wondered if she would inherit such gifts.

If not now, then when? Katherine thought to herself. *There's probably a stupid ceremony to get them.*

Heaven knew the coven societies *loved* their ceremonies.

Then she snapped out of her thoughts as her mother said, "With LaCroix dead, I need a known representative lord of the were-peacocks. One who will obey my commands to the letter and bring back the were-peacock family from this appalling fall from grace."

Nimestra's eyes widened, but all she did was nod.

The queen paced in front of her. "That person will need to be known in the were-peacock community and knowledgeable about LaCroix's affairs, both so they do not commit the same mistake as he and so they continue in his place with very little fuss. Do you agree?"

Again Nimestra nodded.

The queen continued on, "I don't have time to interview candidates, but I'm also tired of pompous assholes who bring nothing but grief to their communities. Perhaps it's time to put a female in charge?"

The queen turned to Nimestra with a sparkle in her eye. "Do you agree, Nimestra?"

The servant woman's shoulders hunched. If she did agree, she was taking on a challenge no one in their right mind would accept. After all, LaCroix's heir would still have to worry about retribution from the faerie, deal with the ramifications of the tainted moon nectar, cancel their supply lines while losing revenue hand-over-foot, and deal with retribution in the form of small-town justice.

Katherine didn't envy Nimestra's choice. Not that it was much of a choice. With her queen covered in her ascendant's blood, she wouldn't think about turning down the 'offer,' either.

Finally Nimestra nodded and said weakly, "Yes, my queen."

A delighted smile blossomed on the queen's face. "Excellent, welcome to the ruling class, Mistress Nimestra. Announce your position to your people, smooth over feathers in my name, and meet me for a full audit of all were-peacock activities in two days."

"Yes, my queen," Nimestra murmured numbly. There was not much else to say. She had traded her bronze servant's shackles for the silver fetters of a ruler under the Queen of Sandersville's thumb. And she knew it.

Finally the queen stepped away from her and the poor woman was able to make her exit at last.

She fled into the night without a further whisper. Then the queen turned a dark gaze on the second guest in the room.

"Why are you here, Nicern?" the queen asked flatly.

The licorn snorted angrily and said, "I was told that you were handing over my land tonight. Without consultation. That is an act of war!"

The queen all but rolled her eyes. "You were told wrong."

"We will not stand for this!" the licorn shouted. He sounded a tad bit drunk. Katherine winced. It was a well-known fact that the tavern where Trip, the brewmaster, worked was Nicern's home and the home of most of his herd—a pack with a total of five perpetually drunk and angry licorns.

The queen didn't flinch. "As I have told you, no such negotiations have taken place and they will not. The Western Reserve is yours. Those feeding grounds are yours to do with as you will. We wouldn't think of taking of it from you."

The belligerent licorn wasn't hearing a word the queen was saying, though.

He slurred his way through a couple of incomprehensible sentences before Katherine said, "You're so sure that *we* want to take something from you when it is the coven community that has heard that you ally with the were-peacock."

"No!" squeaked the only were-peacock in the room.

"How dare you, you impudent whore!" shouted the leader of the licorns.

Then ice formed on the licorn's horns and fangs and his eyes dulled to a distinct pink color, a sign that the sudden frost in the room was affecting him.

"That is my daughter you speak of, Nicern," the queen whispered in a deadly voice.

The licorn bowed his head, not in anger but in regretful acknowledgement. He might be extremely drunk, but he wasn't suicidal.

"Apologies, girl," he mumbled.

The queen raised a cool eyebrow.

"I'll say again," Queen Leanna said in a tense voice. "Why are you here? State your business, and it had better be convincing enough to show me that you had *nothing* to do with Mr. LaCroix's power-grab, or your carcass will be joining him in the town square on the morrow."

The licorn leader tossed his head with an irritated harrumph, which came out like a wispy neigh.

"Of course I had nothing to do with that irritating piss-sucker's plan," said Nicern disdainfully. "Why would I?"

Tactful he was not. But honest…that he was.

The queen nodded and tapped her bottom lip. "Indeed, why would you? I see no reason for you to join forces with LaCroix."

The licorn leader nodded triumphantly.

"Unless, of course, you suspected your land was being given away to the faerie and came here to challenge that decree," the queen said softly.

This time Nicern *did* neigh in anger. "That's a crock full of shit and you know it, Leanna. I came here first. To you, because I respect you. We know you may be a two-legged sympathizer with a stick up your bum about blood feedings, but you've always been fair."

Katherine blinked at the double insult snugly interjected right beside a compliment. If he had been a man like LaCroix, always aiming to please until he didn't want to and then the daggers came out, she would have said it was deliberate.

But because it was Nicern, and he was drunk higher than two skunks rolling in opium, she would give him the benefit of the doubt. Besides, he probably didn't see it as an insult so much as the plain truth.

Either way, Katherine's mother smiled, her twitching lip indicating that she was fighting the urge to break out in laughter.

I'm glad she found this amusing, Katherine thought while struggling to hold back an impolite yawn, although she very much doubted Nicern would care. He didn't seem the type to be a stickler about manners. Besides, she was bone tired. She'd been up since before dawn and it was now well past dusk. She could have sworn she heard the midnight bell toll an hour ago, but she hadn't been paying too close attention considering how busy she was at the moment. She didn't bother trying to focus on the moon's position in the sky and tell the time; she was too tired to get an accurate reading.

Finally her mother spoke. "It's a good thing I believe you, Nicern."

"Yes, it is," trumpeted the drunk licorn.

Katherine's mom sighed and rubbed her brow. "I've got a headache. You may leave."

The licorn looked confused for a moment but got the message when two guardians none-too-politely crowded him out the door.

Two down, one to go, Katherine thought ruefully as she looked over at the sole remaining petitioner in their home.

The funeral director sniffed and stepped forward to the center of the room. With a disgruntled look at the guardian he considered his adversary and a jerk of the front of his suit jacket to straighten the rumples, he said, "My queen, I came as soon as I could to inform you that the preparations for the ceremony are done. Your eldest daughter, Rose Thompson, lies in a protected outdoor gazebo awaiting your attendance."

The queen closed her eyes and opened them again as if pained. "My attendance?" her mother said numbly.

For the first time the man faltered. "Yes, my queen. Your sister, Sarah Thompson, guards her body, as requested."

If the arrangement annoyed him, it didn't show in his tone.

Finally the queen nodded. "Very well, I will attend to my duties for my eldest daughter. Katherine and I will stand watch as Rose transitions from this world to next on tomorrow's dawn."

Katherine nodded wearily and turned to head outside. She was dead on her feet, but she wouldn't complain about this task—it was her sister, after all.

The queen caught Katherine's shoulder as she attempted to pass by. Turning to her mother with a frown, Katherine watched her mother shake her head.

"No, my dear. Tonight's vigil is not for you. Tonight you rest. When the day has dawned you will walk with me to your sister's final resting place."

Katherine protested, "No, I should be there tonight."

"That is not how it's done," her mother said gently.

"I should be there," Katherine repeated stubbornly, not quite sure why she was arguing, but not quite willing to give up the point. Perhaps it the weariness of the day bearing down on her and making her stubborn. Perhaps it was the hope to see her sister again before another sun rose in the sky, although it certainly wouldn't matter to Rose.

"Go to your bed," said the queen wearily. "Cecily awaits you there. You will see Rose in the morning and be gladder of it."

"And you?" Katherine asked. "When will you rest?"

"I already have," the queen said with a mournful smile. "Your aunt made me while she sneaked out of the house to go to the shop."

Katherine had the grace to blush in embarrassment. "About that?"

Her mother waved a dismissive hand. "I know why you went. It was the right thing to do."

"It was?" echoed Katherine in confusion as she wondered if she had heard her mother correctly.

"You were right to seek the comfort of your blood relative's presence," the queen said. "It is what I did when I first learned of Rose's death."

Katherine grimaced. There was nothing about her aunt that she would describe as comforting, a fact that her mother knew well, because she grinned impishly as she said, "You know there's another side to her, right? A caring side."

"A caring side for *you*, maybe," Katherine pointed out. "She hates everyone else."

"That's just the barrier she erects to protect herself from the world," the queen said.

"Or the world from her," Katherine said, while thinking over Ethan's words about her aunt, his foster mother, kicking him out. And the woman certainly had no overwhelming love for Cecily, either. She treated her more like a house sitter than a daughter.

"I doubt she knows or cares where Cecily is on a day-to-day basis, either," muttered Katherine.

"What was that?" asked her mother as she peered down at her in her concern.

"Ah, nothing, I guess I'll go to bed then," Katherine said in a hesitant voice.

The queen nodded and let her go. Katherine turned around and headed up the stairs. As she ascended to the second floor where her bedroom was, she stopped for a moment and peered over her shoulder. She saw her mother, shoulders straight, heading out the door into the darkness. The funeral director just a few steps behind her.

Pride filled Katherine Thompson. Pride in Leanna Thompson's stance. Pride in her mother's effortless switch from mother to queen and back again without batting an eye.

CHAPTER TWENTY

It had been three days since Rose's death. Three days of mourning. Three days of rattling around a seemingly empty house which was in fact only emptier by one body. With the guardians on constant rotation now *inside* their home, not just outside of it, it certainly hadn't gotten less crowded. But with Rose gone, it felt like a yawning gap that Katherine couldn't fill.

At the moment Katherine was outside meditating. She'd been doing so for the last half-hour, legs crossed in the style that mimicked Native American practices, hands calmly at her waist, head tilted up to catch the last rays of the morning sun before it gave way to the stifling heat of a bright, cloudless afternoon, and her mind in turmoil with emotions. She couldn't think straight. It felt as if her thoughts were racing a mile a minute, and that as soon as she settled on one it was off to the other, and she felt anything but at peace.

Katherine decided that the last twenty minutes of sitting on her ass in the brown grass of fall had been a wash. So she stood up and stared down at Gestap, who reclined by her side with a frown.

"We should do something," she ventured.

"Like what?" said the kobold that currently lay on his back with nothing on but a pair of blue boy's swimming trunks she'd bought out of the pre-teens' section.

Well, she was meditating. He was sunbathing. A ritual he loved to do in his natural form and loathed in his adored second form as a giant toad.

"Like get out of this house and this yard," Katherine muttered while kicking the dirt.

She glared down at the too-relaxed kobold until he peeked open a beady eye.

"Is this you being restless or is there a reason for this excursion?" he asked pointedly.

"You know what?" Katherine said in a huff. "Never mind."

She got up, dusted off her pants, and ran back to the house. Opening the front door in a loud enough huff to make her feel like a child having a temper tantrum, she slammed the door shut and rushed upstairs to her room, to the peace and sanctity of private quarters.

It wasn't Gestap. It really wasn't. It was life. It was the unfairness of living in a society ruled by one class and feeling like it's an injustice but not knowing what to do about it. It was having her older sister die and having a knot of pent up rage in her belly that wouldn't go away. It was her messed-up family, her lack of a wide circle of friends—it was her whole life. Katherine Thompson just felt like she was drowning in a whirlpool of doubt and she couldn't help but be miserable at her own thoughts because…well…what did she have to be miserable about? She was the daughter of a *queen*, the heir to the throne, alive and sane.

Katherine threw herself on her four-poster bed and in a fit of irritation, grabbed her stuffed tiger and lobbed him across the room as hard she could. He hit the bathroom door with a solid *thunk*, and she felt a small corresponding well of happiness for just a moment. It lasted no longer than that, because her door opened a second later with no fanfare or knock. Staring up at her mother, Katherine glared.

She was never angry with her mother. Ever. They weren't best friends like she and Rose had been, but Katherine knew her mother cared for her just as much as she did for Rose. She was there when Katherine needed her to detangle her hair, she was there when Katherine brought her first pet home—a fire snail her mother promptly made a cage for out of old Styrofoam packing boxes—and she was there to bake a surprise cake for Katherine when she came home crying over breaking up with Ethan and wouldn't even tell her why.

But as Katherine stared up at her, she didn't see her mother. She saw the queen.

And that was a different person entirely. For Katherine's entire life there had existed a dichotomy between how she acted around and approached her mother in the public eye—at town events, human christenings, public openings, compact signings between the fae communities and the like—and how she approached her in private when they baked cookies, painted bedrooms, looked up vacation rentals in the county over and stuff like that.

There was almost never a day when her mother, as queen overtook her role as mother in their home. But Tuesday—the day Rose had died, the day everything had changed—had been such a day, and it looked like today was another.

"And what about Rose?" she asked, exasperated. "Are we just going to forget about her? That she was killed, even murdered?"

"I told you," the queen said quietly. "Our preliminary investigations and all evidence point to the contrary. I'm sorry, my love, but it was an accident, a tragic one, and we're just going to have to live with that."

"That's bullshit and you know it!" Katherine said.

"Katherine Jane Thompson, you *will* watch your tongue."

Katherine gritted her teeth to keep from another outburst. "Surely, Mother, you can see that it was no natural cause."

Her mother sighed and raised her hand to rub a furrowed brow. "What proof do you have, Katherine? What do you know that half a dozen investigators don't?"

That was the trouble, though. Katherine *didn't* have any proof. Only suspicions. And suspicions weren't enough to convict anyone or anything in court, not her mother's and certainly not in any high queen's.

Shoulders slumped, Katherine mumbled, "Nothing."

The queen lifted her daughter's downtrodden face to meet her own. "I would do anything to bring Rose back and I would move Heaven and Hell to avenge her if something or someone had wronged her. But there's nothing to avenge. Now it is time for us to move past this and remember her in death as she was in life. We want to *celebrate* Rose, not let her death fester in us like an open wound that won't heal."

Katherine didn't say anything. She *couldn't* say anything. The burial ceremony was done. Her sister was in the ground. But nothing about this felt right. Nothing.

Emotions crossed Katherine's face until she finally settled on one—resignation.

Finally Katherine did the only thing she could do: she shook off her mother, rolled over on her bed, said, "Fine," and promptly stuck in her headphones.

Her mother didn't move from the bed. When Katherine still wouldn't look at her from where she stared adamantly at the walk, the queen tugged off the headphones Katherine wasn't really listening to anyway and cleared her throat.

"Yes?" Katherine asked while managing to imbibe one word with both resentment and loathing.

"It's a hard time for us all, dear. But you need to leave the house and get back to your life. As such, I'm letting you know now…you will be going to school tomorrow," said her mother.

Katherine looked over at the Queen of Sandersville, her jaw on the floor.

"You're kidding, right?"

"The Thompson clan must always set an example. You're going," said her mother.

Katherine slid off the bed and sat in a slump on the floor.

"Just what I need," she muttered disdainfully. "More high school."

Her mother sighed and walked around the bed to see her face-to-face. She would never roll across the bed—no, not her mom. But still, the queen did kneel down in front of her daughter in her linen suit skirt and take one of Katherine's trailing hands.

"With the right to rule comes responsibilities, Katherine," she said.

Katherine fought hard not to roll her eyes. "Yeah, like the responsibility to take a human teacher's crap and be criticized for every move I make."

Her mother dropped her hand and reached up to tip Katherine's chin up with her fingertip.

"No, dear," she said. "You're confusing responsibility with duty. It is our *duty* to be in the public eye, to set an example and to follow the rules. Because if a queen doesn't conform to her own rules, then anarchy will soon set in."

Katherine scoffed, "I get it. I do. But can you really say that because you don't open your shop every week day and sell at a normal price, the entire town will go to Hell?"

The queen sighed. "You wouldn't think it would, would you? But *yes*. Because if I do, what's to say the baker down the street wouldn't raise his prices twenty cents just because he could? If he did, people would starve."

"And you could punish him."

"Punish him for the crime of making a living for his family? If I raise my prices, he would need to raise his, as would every other business on the main street."

"Punish him for being greedy. Set the guardians on him."

"A queen who rules in fear is no queen at all," her mother replied.

Katherine shifted in unease. She agreed, but silently she wondered how they had gone from her perfect attendance to economic graft in one conversation.

Her mother stood. "It is our *responsibility* to rule the people with honor and with respect. We are Sandersville, and without that responsibility we would be no better than the dark queens."

Katherine's head snapped up. It was the second time she had ever heard her mother refer to the other queens. The ones who ruled with fear and blood. She didn't think it was a coincidence that both of those times had happened within a week of Rose's death and both of their lives turning upside down.

She opened her mouth and closed it.

Finally, Katherine said, "I need a break. I'm going for a ride."

Scrambling up, Katherine fled her room like the hounds of Hell were on her heels, flew down the hardwood stairs and out the door with her hair streaming back from her face as she hurried to their *other* barn, conveniently kept across the property from where Gestap lived in his hovel-like abode on the edge of the swamp. She wasted no time in saddling Black Fire. The only steed they 'owned,' although it was more like *he* owned *them*.

As she led him out of the stall, Black Fire snorted in disdain. Pushing his wings out irritably once in a while.

"You're ready to fly, huh, boy?" she cooed to him.

"Well, so am I," she said as she tightened the last saddle strap between his massive wings. Hopping up from a mounting block, she grabbed his reins and mounted. With a swift kick in Black Fire's ribs they were off. As he broke into fast trot toward the open fields, she leaned forward in anticipation. This was the best part of her day. The rising sun at her back as he spread his massive wings and they took flight.

And for a moment Katherine forgot her worries as she flew through the skies.

CHAPTER TWENTY-ONE

The next day's dawn rose with Katherine trudging back from her morning duties in the swamp. As she walked-in the through the mudroom, careful to remove her thick, all-weather galoshes that doubled as swamp gear when she needed to take Gestap out, she sprayed down her lower legs with the hose. Trying to get off as much as mud and dirt as she could. This morning had been a particularly messy affair, with her not paying attention to her surroundings in the swamp. Although 'not paying attention' was putting it lightly. She had been completely oblivious to the fact that the log to the right of her skiff was, in fact, moving, and when she had thrust the end of her pole into the swamp floor in order to vault to the platform as always, she had almost lost a leg in the process.

The waiting alligator had reared up in a flash of serrated teeth and a gaping maw. It was only thanks to quick work by Gestap that had involved the kobold leaping straight at the alligator to push him aside that had saved her life. The powerful alligator's jaws had ended up snapping closed on the strong pole, which once inside the gator's mouth might as well of been a flimsy stick, and she had fallen forward with a hard *thud* onto the wooden surface of the platform. The fall had left her body half-in, half-out of the swamp, which she had quickly corrected as she scrambled forward and stood.

Katherine remembered her heart racing in her throat when she had first turned around to look for Gestap. In his toad form he was just as vulnerable to a gator's bite as she was with his moist, thin skin. But, to her relief, Gestap was just as aware of that fact as she was because she turned to see him scuffling the four-foot long alligator not as a toad, but as a kobold. And he was definitely holding his own. Gestap had transformed his naturally curved nails into sharpened spikes of bone and his teeth protruded from his mouth like a creature from a nightmare with dozens of thick, pointy fangs lining the interior and exterior of his mouth.

The water of the swamp had swirled and splashed as the alligator and kobold wrestled for domination in the early morning hours. Katherine had known that Gestap wouldn't let go of the punctured grip he had on his prey. He couldn't because that would leave his foe free to swerve and come at him from another direction with its powerful jaws. Instead he drove his clawed right hand into the alligator's side over and over again while holding on to him with his left and tearing at his soft underbelly with a ravenous mouth. Before two minutes had passed, the swamp water all around the platform had turned red with blood and an exhausted Gestap emerged victorious from its murky depths. With swift kicks he swam over to the platform and pulled himself up out of the water with a helping hand from Katherine.

Carefully avoiding his still razor-sharp claws, she helped him to stand when he insisted on "greeting his defeated foe with proper decorum," and they watched as the dead carcass slowly rose to the surface in the rippling water and a group of ravenous alligators rose soon after to feast on their fallen brethren.

Katherine had released Gestap's hand with a shudder and said, "Can we go home now?"

Her voice was a little forlorn, a little lost. Perhaps sensing her disturbed nature, Gestap didn't tease or prod her on her misstep. He simply said, "Sure," and pushed the skiff that bumped against the platform with each lapping wave of blood-infused water around to the other side so that she could get in safely.

And that had been her morning. So now Katherine was furiously spraying down her muddy pants. Turning off the water hose with a yank of the knob, she tossed the hose back out the door of the mudroom and into the yard, then quickly stripped herself of her pants and her jacket. Stuffing both into a bucket that the family kept in the room specific for clothes too far gone to be used again and would be incinerated the first chance they got, Katherine raced into the house where the heat was sure to be on, leaving the uninsulated mudroom behind in her wake.

With a sigh, Katherine got ready for class just as if it was any other day. As if her life hadn't fallen apart like hell in a hand basket, as if her mother wasn't more distant than ever—except for the moments she felt that she and Katherine needed to have a heart-to-heart, which lately seemed to revolve around which fae leaders in the community were trustworthy and which needed to be quietly offed, and she hadn't seen anyone else since the funeral.

It was customary to leave the grieving family members in peace unless the widow or widower made special accommodations to assure mourners they were welcome in the queen's home. Mother had opened up the house to a mourning day for one day and their refrigerator was now so packed with casseroles that Katherine was stocking the overflow in the cool basement downstairs. Naturally a chilly climate, it had turned downright frosty in the last week. Which was how Katherine knew that no matter how busy her mother tried to make herself and no matter how unaffected she appeared with a mask of dutiful mourning on her face, she wasn't all right. Something was terribly wrong with the Queen of Sandersville. If Katherine thought a mother-daughter heart-to-heart, their third in three days, would help, she would have marched into her mother's office and forced her to sit down. But her mother was a pro at shutting down unless she wanted to open up, and so far the only person she seemed inclined to tolerate in that regard was her only sister, Katherine's aunt.

Katherine grimaced and wondered as she raced back down the stairs in fresh clothes for school and pulling a comb through her damp hair as she went. *Where in the world is Aunt Sarah? She went to fetch Rose's remains days ago, and never came back. Even for her that was strange. She missed Rose's fucking funeral. I hope wherever she is, it was darn important.*

With a sigh, Katherine dragged open Marigold's creaky door. As she prepared to hop into the Beetle's old interior, her eyes happened to glance up and land on Rose's brand-new car. For a moment Katherine considered it and pushed the thought out of her mind in disgust. Her sister was barely dead; she wasn't going to rummage through her stuff like some hunter foraging for gold.

"We'll deal with Rose's car and her room when we deal with it," Katherine said while pushing her sunglasses down off her head and onto the bridge of her nose while tossing her backpack onto the cracked leather of Marigold's passenger seat. With little time left to lose, she pushed the garage door opener impatiently, backed out of the garage, and zoomed off toward school.

Or, well, zoomed off in Marigold style. Which was about forty-five miles per hour tops on a *good* day. Damn, she missed that SUV.

When she got to the middle and high school that sat on the edge of the town, Katherine leaned back into the seat of her parked car and wished she had to be anywhere but here. She had arrived twenty minutes before homeroom because Marigold had actually made a pretty respectable effort today. Now she pushed the glasses back from her face and stared moodily out of the windshield. She could see the destroyed classroom windows from where she was parked. They had been covered with plastic sheets taped to the sides of the brick wall and all the glass had been cleaned away. Katherine grimaced and got out of the car, thinking, *I better get in there. It's better to know* before *homeroom if I've been expelled or not.*

She didn't think there was much chance of her escaping punishment. At all. After all, an entire classroom had seen her call upon the fierce winds and blast out the windows with her neat trick. They might not be sure *how* she did it, but that wouldn't stop them from yammering away to the nearest assistant principal in the hopes that the 'emotional turmoil' might get them out of a midterm or two. Humans were nothing if not practical in that way. She had to admire them for their ingenuity. But right now she felt like cursing her damned luck. It wasn't as if she *wanted* to go to school. What she wanted was one less problem on her plate and one less adult haranguing her. If she knew the administration at this school, it was one wish that would definitely remain unfulfilled.

With the wind in her face, she walked by whispering crowds of students with her head held high and wished she was anywhere but here. No one tried to stop her, but she could feel their stares behind her back and whispers like sharp pinpricks in her mind. At that moment she would have given her right leg for a true guardian. A protector. A paladin. A person who would have her back through good times and bad.

Her mother didn't have one. Her sister certainly hadn't had one.

Every high queen had a paladin of sorts sworn to them. Mid-level witches and prospective queens were lucky if they could share the guardian for their principality. Katherine had heard that the powerful queens of the city courts had their own *warlocks* that attended to their safety. Then she burst out laughing—she couldn't help it. Rose had a warlock by her side and look what good it did her.

For a moment the whispers halted. Shocked silence followed. The students probably thought it was highly improper that she was laughing or that she had gone momentarily insane. The truth of the matter was that none of the students she went to school knew her. Not the *real* her. It wasn't that she pushed them away so much as kept to herself. It wasn't that she was mean, either. In fact, she went out of her way to protect the weaker kids in the hallways. But more often than not, her powers tended to explode out with destructive force. And most people, a select few of crazies not included, liked to steer well clear of that.

When she made it into the cool hallway lit by overhead fluorescent lights, she found that it was blessedly empty. Katherine swiftly made her way down the hall to the small side office that housed her assistant principal. The one who tended to like her the most and understood her quiet misfit nature. Just as she reached forward to turn the door handle, it opened in front of her with a *whoosh* and out walked Connor with surprise plastered on his face.

"Katherine?" he said, making her name a question.

"Connor?" she said in reply, unconsciously mimicking his inflection.

"What are you doing here?" they both blurted out at once.

Katherine blinked. "Figuring out my punishment for that *incident* a few days ago. You?"

He shrugged. "Got in trouble with Ms. Gorsachieky again."

Katherine narrowed her eyes and crossed her arms. "I don't know why you insist on provoking her. You know it's against the rules to read another witch or warlock's mind."

"She can't prove that I'm doing anything of the sort," Connor whined.

Katherine snorted. "You know and I know, that she's upset for a reason."

"Well, if she was *truly* upset about the 'fantasies' I see," Connor answered while raising his fingers and making bunny ears to emphasize his sarcasm, "then she would acknowledge full-out that I read her mind and have me suspended. Instead she sends me to this assistant principal's office every chance she gets."

The last sentence was said in a tone of outright disgust.

Katherine breathed out deeply. "You know you can't keep accusing her of being a long-lost fascist from the Russian Empire without proof."

"I know what I saw," Connor said, sticking out a petulant lip.

"Whatever," Katherine said, reaching around him and grabbing the door knob to turn the handle and push the door open.

"That reminds me," Connor exclaimed in a hurry, "I didn't mean what are you doing *here*, I meant what are you doing *here*, as in school."

A small smile tugged on Katherine's lip. You couldn't distract Connor from his point for very long.

"I'm here because I have to be," she said simply.

"Damn, Katherine, your sister died," he said in surprise. "Give it a week at least."

Katherine said over her shoulder as she turned the knob on the door and entered the office, "I wish I could."

CHAPTER TWENTY-TWO

Katherine sighed when she walked into the room and saw the secretary's desk was empty and the door to the assistant's principal office was closed. It was a tiny box-like room with the secretary's desk taking up all the space not used as a pathway directly between the door that led to the hallway and the door that led to the assistant principal's office.

For moment, in the empty passageway, Katherine had peace. She drummed her fingers against the plywood of the door that she leaned against and reluctantly pushed herself away from its comforting embrace. Walking the four steps that marked the distance from one door to the other, she raised a fist and knocked resolutely on the door.

"Come in," said a male voice.

Katherine pushed the slightly ajar door open without further invitation. In the slightly larger room that served as his office,

Katherine found Mr. Nielsen standing in the corner and shuffling through some papers beside his file cabinet.

He looked up quickly at her approach and said, "Ah, Ms. Thompson, I've been expecting you."

A solemn look broached his face. A slight smile crossed hers. She happened to find Mr. Nielson to be one of the more approachable administrative officials in the schools. Once or twice she had even come to talk to him on her own accord.

He finished shuffling his papers and rapidly stuffed the sheath in a folder before slamming the file door shut and walking toward his desk.

Gesturing at a chair, Mr. Nielsen said, "Please, sit down."

Katherine promptly took the indicated metal and leather seat that had seen better days. This school was the only one in town for more reasons than one—they couldn't afford to run two school buildings for separate middle school and high school curriculums, although they had a large enough student body to maintain such a quorum if needed.

As Katherine settled in the squeaky chair, she turned calm eyes on Mr. Nielsen, waiting on his pronouncement, whatever it might be. After all, he said he had been expecting *her*, which at the very least, meant he had something to say to her.

Mr. Nielson, for his part, folded his hands and rested his chin on the bridge they formed.

"How are you doing, Katherine?" he asked in a calm tone.

"Fine." Katherine shrugged, wanting to get this over with.

He nodded and reached out for a candy dish. Picking it up, he held it out to her. "Toffee?"

She shook her head quickly. Could he just get on with it? If he gave her a legitimate excuse to leave, she was *gone*. But if her mother heard that she had pressured the human administrator into excusing her from her classes, she'd never hear the end of it. Never mind that Katherine would never do such a thing. Not without a darned good reason, anyway.

"Fine," he said simply while popping a rejected toffee into his mouth. "Let me be blunt. First you became withdrawn in class, then you stormed outdoors to deal with something best left alone, and now this…your has sister passed away."

Katherine frowned but said nothing. The second accusation could use a little bit of clarification from her, but it's not like she understood the phenomenon fully anyway, and Rose's passing was none of his business. But she wasn't going to speak up and object. Mainly because this conversation was going exactly the way she wanted.

"But I don't think the answer is to sink into sullen resentment," the man said.

"Neither do I," blurted out Katherine. She was hoping this was her chance. Here was the moment he said leave school and clear you thoughts for a few days. She leaned forward in eager anticipation of those words.

But as Mr. Nielson continued talking, she rapidly got a sinking feeling in her heart. "So I'm recommending that you take on three counseling sessions a week with our school practitioner."

Katherine sat up abruptly and her jaw dropped. This was *so* not what she wanted.

The man continued to move his dreadful toffee around in his mouth. She was beginning to wonder what she'd ever seen in him in the first place—this announcement was tantamount to the greatest betrayal.

Nervously Katherine cleared her throat. "Mr. Nielsen...I know you want to help. I'll be more active in class, I promise. I don't need *counseling*."

The man smiled. "I'm sure you think you don't, but it can help to talk over your feelings with a qualified professional."

"I don't *want* to talk about my feelings with someone else, professional or otherwise. I'm fine on my own. If I need to, I've got Gestap," Katherine interjected.

The man wrinkled his nose at the mention of the kobold's name. "As suitable as Mr. Gestap may be, Ms. Florence will be better."

"I'm sure she would, but I refuse..."

He cut her off as he said, "I've already spoken to the queen, who supports this measure, Ms. Thompson. You will be going to counseling three times a week starting this afternoon during your physical education class. I hope this, along with the coven guidance that Ms. Florence might be able to give, will be of help to you."

Katherine snapped her mouth closed with an audible *click* of her teeth. It seemed as though he already made his decision.

"Fine," she said in a huff as she stood and thrust the squeaking chair back with a scrape across the floor. "I'll go."

"Very good, Katherine," he said placidly from where he sat, still sucking on that dratted toffee.

Katherine sniffed and walked to the door. Yanking it open, she turned back to Mr. Nielsen and said, "Just so you know...Ms. Florence is a fucking white witch with the powers of a bunny and the knowledge of a toadstool. She couldn't lead herself out of a closet, let alone someone else."

And with that Katherine left a flabbergasted assistant principal behind and rushed out into the hallway. As she did so, she pulled her sunglasses down from atop her head and hastily pulled them over her eyes just as the homeroom bell rang. It was a good thing wearing sunglasses in the middle of broad daylight was in fashion with the teens at school. She gave no small thanks to the lamia, the blood-drinking fae creatures that humans liked to refer to as vampires after some human archetype or other, for that measure.

Slinking into homeroom, Katherine crossed her arms and watched a substitute teacher begin to scribble notes on Ms. Peabody's board for first-period class. Katherine knew it was for them because she had chalked "First Period Instructions" in cursive at the very beginning.

Slouching as she watched the woman, Katherine waited for her turn around and face the room, but she never did. She just kept scribbling what looked like paragraphs of instructions on the board. Katherine began to feel damned sorry for Ms. Peabody's first period class.

She looked around as the surrounding students began to exchange whispers between friends. If they were talking about her, she didn't care. Today sucked. Not only had she gotten sucker-punched into counseling, but she *still* had to go to school. Whoever had said life wasn't fair had been prescient with the knowledge from the gods.

"Life really isn't fair," Katherine muttered to herself darkly.

"You're telling me," said a young a man she didn't know. He'd been eavesdropping. When he saw the frown on her face, he quickly turned away.

"Jeez, Katherine," said Connor as he plopped down in a vacant seat in front of her. "Scare away *all* of the potential boyfriends, why don't you."

"I'm not in the mood, Conner," she grouched.

"Not for *you*," he said in disgust. "I meant for me."

Katherine lowered the sunglasses with a tip of her finger and raised an eyebrow. She gave Connor a sarcastic look.

"What?" Connor said with a shrug. "He was cute."

"If you're into the surfer-boy type," she said.

"You know I am," Connor said proudly, his dusting of freckles standing out on his face and halo of red hair smoothly slicked back across his lily-white forehead and blue eyes.

She rolled her eyes but grinned. It was true. Connor made no secret of his preferences and was generally very forthright about what he did and didn't like, potential boyfriends included.

Speaking of which, Katherine said in confusion, "Why haven't you asked him out?"

Connor blinked his baby-blue eyes at her. "Because I don't know if he likes me, duh."

Katherine glared. "You're a telepath, *find out*."

This time it was Connor who rolled his eyes. "You know I don't do that with people I care about."

"Thanks," grouched Katherine in a huff, remembering all the times Connor had invaded *her* privacy.

Connor quickly reached out and patted her arm. "Oh, don't be such a doll. You know I think well of you. Which is why I *have* to see what's going on in that head of yours to ward off disaster."

"Uh-huh," Katherine said dryly. "Nice save."

Connor smirked. "I meant to tell you earlier, by the way. I...I think you did a really good job with whatever that was, and you know, whatever you are, I support you."

Katherine leaned forward in disbelief. "*Whatever* I am?"

Connor shifted uncomfortable. "Oh, come on Katherine. You and I know we've never seen a witch or warlock with powers like yours in the town before. You're different. Almost otherworldly."

Katherine sat back, disturbed as she bit her lip. She couldn't say he was wrong. But she didn't want to admit he was right, either.

"Anyway," Connor quickly exclaimed in an obvious effort to change the subject, "where's that dratted cousin of yours?"

Katherine blinked and looked around the classroom. Connor was right. Cecily wasn't here...*again*. And this time Katherine hadn't seen her in the last couple days.

"I don't know," she said, mystified, just as the bell rang to transition to second period.

CHAPTER TWENTY-THREE

Katherine tried calling Cecily as she hurried between classes with no answer. By the time the end of second period rolled around, she was officially freaked out at not being to reach her. Deciding that her cousin's safety took priority and she *really* didn't want to be around anyway for a third-period physical education class held in a counselor's office, she skipped out of school and headed across town.

To—where else?—the family shop.

Rushing in the front door, Katherine looked around and her shoulders drooped in astonishment. The door had been unlocked, yes, but it wasn't Cecily who greeted her but the store manager who came in when she was off-duty at the local ice cream shop.

Forcing a smile, Katherine greeted her, "Natalie, hey. What's up?"

Natalie finished wrapping a satchel for a customer and slid it into the elderly man's hand with a gracious smile before she looked over at Katherine with a sunny smile. "Hey, Katherine! I wasn't expecting anybody else in for a few hours. Are you taking over your mom's shift?"

"Uh, no," Katherine said nervously. "She's not on her way, is she?"

The siren with bright blue hair took a quick look at her watch. "Not as far as I know. I've got two more hours on the clock."

Katherine nodded nervously. "Great, have you seen Cecily, by any chance?"

Natalie shrugged. "Not since last week when she and I were on shift together."

Katherine's shoulders slumped. Another dead end.

"All right, well, I'm going to go see if I can find her," Katherine said while backing out of the shop.

"Sure," Natalie said, puzzled.

As Katherine reached for the door handle behind her from memory Natalie said, her ink-black eyes unchanging, "Katherine?"

"Yes?" Katherine paused.

"I'm sorry for your loss."

A flash of pain crossed Katherine's face, but she took the sympathy as she'd been taught to—graciously. "Thank you, Rose will be missed."

And she would be...forever. But the thought of Rose's memory did nothing but bring up anguish in Katherine's mind. Nothing about Rose's death was natural. Nothing about the ceremony they had performed over Rose's remains had been traditional. Nothing felt right about her passing. It was like a raw open wound in Katherine's heart that she was absolutely sure she couldn't heal. How do you heal when you can't find closure? When no one else around you have sought out closure and no one else seemed to care?

Least of all the woman that Katherine counted on the most in her life to find out the how and why, the woman who had given birth to them, the woman who was their queen.

With a rueful sigh, Katherine pushed open the shop door and walked outside.

Standing on the sidewalk, she called Cecily's cellphone twice.

Growling in frustration when she got no answer and none of the texts she'd sent over the past two hours had been answered, Katherine decided to do something she had promised herself she'd never do.

She was going to go see Ethan Nestor. He, above all others, would know where his foster sister was at all times. The bond between them was as strong as the bond between siblings.

"Even stronger," snorted Katherine as she hopped into Marigold, "considering that Rose and I fought like cats and dogs all the time."

Katherine thought she knew where he'd be today. So she turned the key in the ignition and headed over to the mechanic's shop where, the last time she'd checked, Ethan had a part-time job.

Getting out the car was the hardest thing Katherine did that day. She almost turned the Beetle around and gunned it out of there. But when Ethan walked out of the door with a rag trailing between his fingers and oil on his face, she had no choice. He had seen her.

Getting out of the safety of Marigold and walking over, she stuffed her hands in her back pockets and rocked back on her feet away from Ethan.

He was quiet, contemplative, waiting for her to speak. He had always been able to outwait her when he chose.

Finally she sighed and said, "There's only one reason I'm here."

"The orb's fine," Ethan said abruptly with a shrug. "I gave it to Ceidian and watched as he started the distribution network that would slowly feed the remaining power back into his people."

Surprise flowed through Katherine. Of all the things for him to bring up, she hadn't thought that would be the first. But she knew Ethan. When he had a job to do or a responsibility to maintain, he did it. Without fuss and unrelentingly. Which was why she'd come to him first about Cecily. He considered her cousin and his foster sister *his* responsibility, as Cecily's birth mother was always away on one mission or another. It was Ethan who had made sure Cecily ate when they lived in the same house; it was Ethan who had given bullies—warlock, fae, or human—black eyes when they messed with Cecily; and it was Ethan who kept tabs on her every day.

It wasn't that Cecily was flighty. It was that she was prone to fainting spells as a consequence of her prophetic witch's gift. She used it sparingly, but as she had grown, the negative effects of using her gifts had worsened year by year. At first it was just an extra bout of hunger when she was young. But now Katherine knew Cecily could be laid out with migraines for a day if she used her gift too much.

She felt a pain of regret at asking Cecily to use it to find Rose as she flashed back on what Cecily had said: *The black thorn.*

But Katherine knew no one else in town with her sister's gift, and her grief over Rose's death had been so fresh that she hadn't thought about the consequences.

Taking a deep breath, Katherine said, "That's good. Really good. I'm sure the queen will have Ceidian's actions monitored tightly."

Ethan nodded. "Yeah, she sent over representatives already."

"Great," Katherine hurried to say, "but that's not why I'm here."

"Oh?" Ethan said thoughtfully as he rubbed a spot of oil from his hands. Her mind remembered him rubbing that same spot months ago when he'd splashed paint on it trying to help her give Marigold a new look. It hadn't really worked—the makeover, that is. Marigold had a tendency to absorb any paint colors she didn't like, a legacy of her days as the former ride of a traveling salesman with the magical gift of living art. It was a pain in the ass, as far as Katherine was concerned, because Marigold actually seemed to *like* looking like a diseased stray cat with orange tiger stripes.

Katherine huffed out noisily, trying to clear her head before any other uncomfortable memories flashed over her. Memories of when she and Ethan had been on better terms. Flashes of better days went through her mind. For a moment all Katherine wanted to do was rush over to him and get one, caring hug out of this craptastic day. But she scuffed her boots on the floor and resisted the urge to go over to him as he waited patiently. She wouldn't go over and let him into her life again. She just needed to find out about Cecily and then she would *leave*.

Katherine had thought she'd gotten over her hurt, but she hadn't. Every time she came into Ethan's presence the memories emerged, both the good and the bad. And the bad? Well, they were pretty bad. At least for a teenage girl facing the first guy she'd had an actual flat-out crush on. Because Ethan had broken up with *her*. Because he had left her after a moment she never wanted to talk about and a night that didn't end well for either side. She had ended that night in tears in the swamp. Crying on Gestap's slimy shoulder and thinking her world had ended. When he hadn't returned her calls, ignored her texts, and ditched school for the entire semester afterwards, she had *known* her life was ending.

Ethan had been her first boyfriend. Her first kiss. Her first love.

Now he stood across from her with carefully blank eyes and waited for her to voice why she was here. And all of sudden Katherine was angry. She didn't exactly know what it was she was angry about. She wasn't sure if it was the hurt, the pain, the rage, or the sorrow, but she knew one thing. She could feel in it her bones that there was one thing she had never done after Ethan had broken up with her that she desperately wanted to do now.

Now she would get some satisfaction for that. With no warning she raced up to Ethan, but not for a hug. She slapped him so hard across his face that the imprint of her hand on his cheek could be clearly seen on his fair skin. He didn't retaliate as his head snapped back.

He simply rubbed his jaw and said softly, "I deserved that. At least, if that's what I think it was about."

She glared and squared her shoulders. "It probably was."

Ethan clenched his jaw. "If you'd just let me explain…"

"No, I think you said enough that night," she said spitefully.

As she swung back for another hit, he caught her hand harshly in his own.

"Fine. But don't think I'm going to let you slap me again."

Frowning, she stepped back while jerking her hand free.

"Fine," she snapped.

He sighed and ran a finger through his hair. "Why are you here, Katherine?"

She shuffled her feet.

"Really, tell me why. And don't tell me you came all the way down here to slap me across the face. You may be feeling bitchy, but you're not vindictive."

"I'm not so sure that was a compliment."

"Wasn't meant to be," he said, crossing his arms defiantly.

Reluctantly, she said, "I was looking for Cecily. I didn't see her this morning in class."

"What do you mean you 'didn't see her'?" he said tightly.

"I looked for her in homeroom and then I realized I haven't seen her since that night at the house," she said, trailing off.

"Go on?"

"Well, I thought she was with her mom or you. But Aunt Sarah's been gone, I haven't seen hide nor hair of her, and when Cecily wasn't in class I came here," Katherine said weakly. "She's not answering her cell phone, either."

"Dammit!" Ethan cursed while throwing the rag to the ground. "I knew I couldn't trust that bitch to watch over her."

"Who?" Katherine said, confused.

"Your aunt," snapped Ethan as he tugged out his cellphone and proceeded to dial some numbers. Cecily's phone, presumably.

"Why would you ever trust Aunt Sarah to take care of Cecily?" Katherine asked, genuinely shocked.

"She insisted on it," Ethan said tightly, "and Cecily backed her up on it. Said they had witches' stuff to do for two or three days and would be out of contact. Cecily made me promise to give her some peace while they went through it."

His phone rang and rang with no answer. Ethan began dialing through his messages, but from his tense shoulders Katherine could tell he found nothing.

Katherine felt some pity for him. Cecily had been Ethan's foster sister before Aunt Sarah blew a gasket and kicked him out. Long story. But suffice it to say that not just their romantic relationship that imploded six months ago in July. Her aunt was a pretty horrible mother *and* guardian. Ethan still watched out for Cecily, though.

"So she's been gone with Aunt Sarah for three days?"

Ethan turned furious eyes on her. "Gone? Gone where? They were supposed to be at the local coven meeting hall."

Katherine shook her head. "According to Mom, Aunt Sarah had to take care of something out of town."

Ethan closed his eyes in horror and then opened them again. "We have to find Cecily."

"All right, where else could she be?" asked Katherine.

"Maybe the house," he muttered. "I was going to take a jacket by yesterday in fact. She left it with me over the spring. Went by the house, but it was dark, so I assumed they were still at the coven hall."

Katherine nodded. "Then let's check the house first. Sometimes Aunt Sarah checks in there before letting anyone know she's arrived back in town."

Ethan said thoughtfully, "You know, I passed the school along the way there. Looked like a tornado had been through it."

She looked away, guilty.

He didn't miss it. "That was you?"

"Maybe."

He sighed. "Of course it was. And Rose—did the same thing happen with her? Losing control of a gift? Maybe it was Derrick's fault."

"We don't know, actually," Katherine said darkly. "No one knows exactly why she died. Cecily, Cecily was supposed to help me find out why Rose died. If it was deliberate, then I *will* kill the person who did this to her."

"You've never killed anyone before."

"Actually, I have."

He looked at her askance.

"Fourth grade, remember?"

He chuckled. "That's right, you decapitated that piece of crap. Well, he had it coming…attacking Cecily like that. It was a good thing the sheriff was able to prove you were protecting her. Even your mother couldn't have stopped them from arresting you for murdering a warlock."

Katherine shrugged uncomfortably. She hadn't even told Ethan that it wasn't her doing, but rather her riders'. Everyone assumed that she had some weird-awesome fighting ability, even her mother. Only Cecily, and now the whole homeroom, knew what she really called down with her witch's gift.

"So," said Ethan softly, "what happened to Rose, and where's Cecily?"

"We find Cecily, we can keep trying to find out what happened to Rose," she said.

Shivering, Katherine continued, "I just hope she's all right. Something just doesn't feel right."

Ethan nodded. "I hear you. If you want to leave Marigold parked in the lot, we can drive over to the house in my car."

Katherine nodded, did as he suggested, and hopped in. As they drove along, she said, "I'm going to try her one more time."

She dialed again.

Immediately they heard Cecily's distinctive ringtone in the car. Frowning, Katherine and Ethan looked at each other, and then he pulled over to the side of the road.

"It's coming from the trunk," Ethan explained.

Turning off the car, he hurriedly unbuckled his seat beat and raced to the trunk. Katherine did the same. Hurrying together, they popped open the trunk to find a bright pink cell phone ringing on the floor mat in between some cable hooks. No other sign of any of Cecily's belongings anywhere.

Katherine grabbed the phone and pulled away as Ethan slammed the trunk door down with a frustrated yell. "Dammit, Cecily. Why would you leave your phone somewhere?"

Katherine shut off her phone and quickly entered Cecily's passcode.

"She shared her code with you?" he said, mildly impressed.

"Of course," she said, shifting away from him. She could feel his presence in the air. It was like an electric current between them. Always had been.

If he noticed her shift, he didn't say anything.

"Check her messages and calls," he said.

"Already on it," she muttered with her head down.

Her attention caught on a series of texts that Cecily had received two days ago.

"Listen to this," she called out to Ethan. "'Deliver the specimens within twenty-four hours.' 'One has died, do you wish the other girl to perish, too?' and a final message: 'Come to us or we will take what we want.'"

CHAPTER TWENTY-FOUR

Grimly, Ethan said, "Let's get to the house."

They got back into the car and wasted no time rushing up the steps of the old stone manor that Aunt Sarah had repossessed, literally, from a gang of ghouls and made into their home.

Fishing a key out from his pocket, Ethan unlocked the door and they walked into a clearly empty home. Light dust gathered, and Aunt Sarah's giant pet salamander had left a trail of poop from one end of the foyer to the other. Something neither Cecily nor her mother could stand to walk over. The minute they stepped through the door it would have been cleaned up.

"Big surprise," Ethan said darkly. "She isn't here."

"Who? Cecily?" Katherine asked.

"Her mother," Ethan said bitterly. "Some people aren't cut out to be mothers, and I have to say she's one of the few that I'd wholehearted agree is one of those people."

"She's pretty standoffish, but she cares," Katherine objected almost automatically. That was her blood aunt he was talking about, after all.

"If was just the fact that she travels alone for weeks at a time hunting demons, I wouldn't have mentioned it," Ethan said gruffly. "But it isn't."

"What do you mean?" she asked as they slowly made their way into the living room.

Ethan walked over to Cecily's favorite part of the house—the corner that housed her baby grand piano, Aunt Sarah's only concession to Cecily's obvious love of music. She had said when she presented Cecily with the instrument that the sounds of the piano was the only live music she could stand and Cecily wouldn't be playing anything in the house, even though she was also gifted with the cello, flute, and harpsichord. Cecily had been so happy to receive the gift that she would have agreed to anything in that moment.

Katherine swallowed as she opened up the cover and trailed her fingers along the pristine keys.

"What did you mean, Ethan?" she prodded gently as she turned around to look at him pacing the room.

Ethan looked at her and then said slowly, "Did Cecily ever tell you about how many times Aunt Sarah would call her weak and pitiful? Make her practice over and over with a practice sword until her arms were blue from bruises and her fingers were so stiff that she couldn't play the piano for a week?"

Katherine frowned. "She might have mentioned something. I think she said Aunt Sarah just wanted to toughen her up. Make sure she could defend herself."

"She wanted to do more than that. She wanted to *break* Cecily."

"Break her?" whispered Katherine horrified.

Ethan snorted disdainfully. "They were as different as cats and dogs. I honestly don't know how something as sweet and kind as Cecily came from *that*. Which is why we need to get her back."

Katherine nodded. "I think we need to search the house at the very least."

Ethan agreed. "You take the top floor. I'll take the main floor and the basement. Meet back here?"

She nodded and headed up stairs, pausing to watch him head into the basement. In the fifteen minutes of opening every room door, checking every closet and bathroom, and even peering out the windows, she didn't find any sign of her cousin.

Rushing back down to the main floor with a frustrated growl, Katherine found Ethan back in the living room.

"Nothing?" she asked.

"Nothing," he replied glumly.

"Now what?" she said, throwing up her arms. "I thought her mother would be here and she's not. There's no sign of Cecily or even where she went. How do we track her down if we have no idea where to go?"

Ethan tilted his head in thought. "I may have an idea. Where's the cell phone?"

Katherine raised an eyebrow. "I left it in the car."

He walked out of the room without another word. When he returned she was sitting on the couch and wringing her hands anxiously.

"You think we should tell my mother?"

"I think we should have some definite proof of where she went first," Ethan said firmly.

Katherine nodded.

She watched him place himself in the middle of the room. Carefully he lowered the pink cell phone to the ground between his feet. Then he was still. Looking straight at the ground with his hands by his side and his hair shielding his face.

Before she could call out, she felt his magic rise and saw it emerge. A pool of light appeared under his feet with thin tendrils of light emerging from the surface. The tendrils reached out like vines and struck out to hit multiple points in the room. And then they all reversed from their various points on the wall to hit one spot: the surface of the bright pink cell phone.

"What's going on?" Katherine asked.

"It's going to show us the last place Cecily had a real live conversation on or near this piece of junk," Ethan advised her.

Katherine was beginning to think he was projecting his anger in more ways than one, but she calmly watched the light show. Hoping it could tell them something about where Cecily had gone.

Slowly she became amazed. Because light filtered out of the beam from the phone and slowly transformed the vision of what they were seeing everywhere in the room. The living room slowly transformed into a place she knew well. The shop—the ceiling, the walls, the glass jars, the plants, the cash register, the door. It was all there.

"Wow," she murmured as she stood up.

He looked up at her with a grin after a moment. "It's going to take a few minutes more to get the history to appear. It's a bit like accessing a download file server and regurgitating the memory."

She blinked at him. "I have no idea what you said."

He sighed. "Give me two minutes."

She shrugged and turned to stare around herself again in awe. She hadn't know he could do this and she was anxious to see what he meant by 'file server.' Maybe it had something to do with what he was or his heritage. Ethan wasn't a warlock, she knew that much. But they hadn't had an actual conversation about what he was and wasn't before, either—she only knew that he was clearly inhuman and not a warlock. Not for her lack of trying. He had always evaded the topic or outright changed the subject when she brought it up. At the time her mother had hated him because he wasn't a warlock and Katherine had been perfectly happy with her disapproval.

Ethan said in the quiet, "You can use the cell phone now. I don't need its presence while I do this."

Katherine nodded. "I'll check for more messages."

She turned on the pink phone and got to work, but there was nothing more wicked there than the two messages they had seen earlier and a couple hundred texts between Cecily and herself.

"Nothing else," she said, defeated.

Ethan frowned darkly. "What about the ones we were able to read earlier? They both came in two days ago."

"One after the other," she said shakily. "Which means if she left to meet them, then she could be missing as long as forty-eight hours. This isn't good."

"I know," he responded.

"What was Cecily mixed up in?"

241

"I don't know," he said in a fierce tone, "but I'm going to find out."

Katherine nodded. She believed him. Biting her lip, she said, "Your magic. Is it going to call up her last conversation?"

"Not on the phone itself," Ethan said, standing still and glancing at her in surprise. "But it will call up the last few minutes surrounding the time she used the phone."

Then the lines of light from his magic flashed like a strobe light in a club, then they spread out in thick pools of light so that the entire room was bathed in light. Stepping closer to Ethan, Katherine watched as he called up the history of the shop through the aura around them.

"It's like watching a television," she said in wonder. The only difference was that a television had sound.

"But a hell of a lot harder." He grunted in strain as the aura TV flashed back to this morning just as her mother left the shop. They watched as Cecily wandered around straightening object and fulfilling orders when patrons came in. Then, close to eight a.m., when she should have been in homeroom, two things happened. Cecily crouched over in pain for a minute then straightened.

"That must have been when Rose died," Katherine said, "Cecily's always been more sensitive to family than I am."

"And this?"

They watched as two men approached Cecily in the shop. One hung back to deter other people from entering near the door. Cecily watched them nervously. They spoke only for a few minutes before she left with them.

"She didn't even try to fight them!" Ethan cried out in frustration.

 242

"Three of them. One of her," said Katherine. "And all of them from the Other Realm. Even I wouldn't like those odds."

"You noticed that, too?" Ethan asked.

"I'd be blind not to recognize a demon when I saw one," Katherine retorted angrily. She wasn't angry at Ethan. She was angry at the demons who had taken her cousin.

"We need to tell her mother," Ethan said grimly.

Katherine grimaced. "Just what I need. More of Aunt Sarah."

"You and me both," Ethan whispered. "But if there's anyone who can recognize and hunt down a demon, it's Cecily's mother."

Sitting down, Katherine asked, "Now how do we find her?"

Ethan banished the lingering effects of the image and said, "Who do we know that your aunt makes sure to inform of her plans no matter what?"

They looked at each other as Katherine rolled her eyes at the obvious answer. "*My* mother."

Ethan nodded. "Let's go to the queen."

They left her aunt's house without a further word and headed back across town to Katherine's home to explain to the Queen of Sandersville that another of the Thompson line was missing, and this time they could do something about it.

When Katherine walked through the door of her home, she took a deep breath and hoped her mother knew where Aunt Sarah was.

Asking a guardian as she made sure they waved Ethan through, she said, "Where's my mother?"

He answered politely, "Out back, miss. At the gazebo."

Katherine stiffened and directed Ethan to drive around the back of the house. They parked near the door to the mudroom and started walking on the dry grass to the small pavilion-like structure that had housed her sister's remains until three days ago.

When they got close enough, Katherine saw her mother kneeling in prayer with the gemstone necklace of Hecate's blessing in her hand. Sorrow rocketed through her. Her mother had never been a particularly devout discipline of the coven religion before, so to see her at it now told Katherine exactly how much she must be hurting inside from her daughter's demise.

Clearing her throat, Katherine approached the white gazebo, but didn't go up the steps and go inside. She just couldn't. It was like entering a tomb unprepared, she wasn't sure what she would find. If lingering remnants of Rose's spirit would be there. If it would torment her or bring her peace. And she didn't want to find out. She just wanted to find Cecily and go home, avoiding everything and everyone in her life that was making her feel so very miserable.

Her mother's head rose and she stood, slipping the gemstones in the pocket of her dress and smoothly exiting the gazebo.

"Katherine and Ethan," the queen said in surprise, "what are you doing here?"

She left off the word 'together,' but Katherine could hear the subtle disapproval in her voice.

Guess she still doesn't like Ethan that much.

Katherine said in a rush, "We think Cecily's missing, and what's more, we think it's an urgent matter."

The queen frowned and said, "Walk with me."

CHAPTER TWENTY-FIVE

With Ethan and Katherine on either side of her, they walked not toward the house, but closer to the forest with her royal guardians trailing not far behind.

"Your Majesty," Ethan said, his voice dark, "Cecily hasn't attended classes for two days now. Her mother explained that they were going to be in town on coven business and yet, they are nowhere to be found."

Speaking in a less-formal tone, the queen said with familiar warmth and quiet in her voice, "Yes, Cecily and my sister were supposed to have, as you say, coven business, but Sarah's occupation took her elsewhere earlier this week."

Katherine watched Ethan's mouth thin into a line. "And why didn't she say anything?"

"About what?" the queen said coolly.

Ethan's eyes flashed and he didn't back down in the face of his queen. This was his *sister* they were talking about, and Katherine knew that he felt he had the right to know her whereabouts.

"That she was leaving," he said tightly. "I would have watched over Cecily."

"She told *me*," her mother responded, "and I will watch over Cecily."

"Like you watch over Katherine?" Ethan lashed out without thinking.

The queen's eyes widened in surprise and hurt before the emotions on her face wiped away as if they had never been there and Katherine's mother was gone. In her place stood the Queen of Sandersville.

"I think, young man, that it is time for you to leave before I do something I regret," she said.

Her guardians surged forward at some invisible command to grab a hold of Ethan.

"Mother, no!" Katherine said frantically. "He didn't mean it. Besides, he's telling the truth. We can't find Cecily! It's urgent."

"Remove him from my property," sniped the queen, and Ethan could say no more because one of the talents of the guardians was a silencing gift. He was dragged away and Katherine was left to plead for her mother's leniency.

They stood in the middle of the field face-to-face. One with desperate eyes. The other with an immeasurable look of concern.

"Mother, I'm sorry we interrupted you," pleaded Katherine, "but you must listen to reason. Something is gravely wrong with Cecily, and you have to extend all of your resources into finding her."

"I do, do I? And who is queen here?" the queen said angrily.

Katherine briefly closed and re-opened her eyes, "That's not what I meant. I'm just worried."

Finally the queen sighed and rubbed her brow. "If it will ease your fear, Cecily came to me two days ago. She said she was going out of town on her first demonic voyage and she would be back within the week. It was time."

Katherine reared back in shock. "Cecily? On a demon hunt? She'd *never* do that."

"She comes from a long line of demon huntresses. Her father's mother was one and so was her mother's mother and her mother."

Katherine narrowed her eyes. She didn't want to debate lineage with her mother now. Although she was very much aware that the queen's mother and her sister's mother were different individuals. It was why the younger sister was Queen of Sandersville and the older one was not.

"But Mother," Katherine said in exasperation, "you *know* Cecily. You know she's never hunted a thing in her life. Why would she start now? This makes no sense!"

The queen waved a hand. "As I said before, I coddled you and your sister. Sarah has decided it's time that she stopped coddling hers. She let Cecily go to prove that she is worthy of the mantle."

Katherine shook her head adamantly. "Cecily would never do that."

"She did," said her mother. "And you need to follow her example. It is time to take on the full responsibilities of an heir to Sandersville. I'm setting you on coven rotation tomorrow."

"No, Mother!" Katherine wasn't exactly sure if she was protesting her mother's characterization of Cecily or herself. It all felt like too much. She had *never* wanted to be Queen of Sandersville, and now it was all being dumped into her lap.

Her mother's patience wore thin. "You have to grow up sometime, Katherine. You can't stay in the forest with Gestap forever. You must learn to lead, and this is the best way I know how. My word is final."

The queen turned away from her stunned daughter and walked back toward the house.

Katherine fell to her knees on the ground and wondered exactly when her life had gone to hell in a hand basket. With slumped shoulders, she realized that the responsibilities of the town were slowly closing around her throat like a noose and she would never be able to leave Sandersville again...not as long as she lived.

Katherine felt silent tears roll down her face but she didn't wipe them away. She let them dry on her cheeks as she stared at the meadow around her. It was winter, which meant the grass was stiff and dry with brown hues. There was chill in the air and the barest bite of cold in the wind. Yet still she didn't move.

She breathed in and out slowly and she thought of all the times Cecily had come to her rescue when she was all alone in the forest, or dragged out of her room when she was consumed with a new spell. Bright, happy Cecily who always had a smile on her face and a comforting shoulder to lean on.

As one final tear rolled down her cheek Katherine stood. She had made her decision. She wasn't going to wait for her mother to come around. She would find her cousin herself. Quietly she hurried into the house and grabbed a burner cellphone she had hidden in her underwear drawer. Texting Ethan to meet her on the far side of the forest with his car, she packed an overnight bag with jeans, two T-shirts and some sweats to sleep in and went right back out the door.

Not bothering to stop. Even to say goodbye to Gestap, she hurried through the meadow and into the darkness of the forest while the light of day still guided her way. With it being late November, the sun was going down sooner earlier in the day, so she didn't have much time before she lost even the small rays of light that pierced the gloominess of the pine trees all around her.

When she got to the road that bisected the forest behind her home and on the opposite of Gestap's swamp, she breathed a sigh of relief to see Ethan standing by his driver's side door and watching her descend down the slippery bank

Unlocking the doors with a click, he slipped into the car without a word and she quickly threw her bag into the back seat and hopped into the front.

"So what's the plan?" Ethan asked Katherine slowly.

"Find Cecily. That's as far as I got."

A bitter smile crossed Ethan's face as Katherine began to think aloud, "We know Cecily's outside of the town boundaries. But we don't know where. If we could find that out…"

"Already done," Ethan said flatly.

"How?" Katherine asked in shock.

"When your mother kicked me out," Ethan said, "I called in some favors."

Katherine turned in her seat to look at him fully. "What kind of favors?"

Ethan smiled. "I know some trackers a few counties over. They'll find anything for the right price. I figured it was a good second-option if Cecily didn't turn up and your aunt was no help."

Breathless Katherine asked, "So where is she?"

Ethan said, "They saw her heading west on Interstate 20."

Katherine nodded and the said, "Then I guess we're heading the same direction."

Ethan put his hand on the keys in the ignition but didn't turn it on. "There's something else."

"What?" Katherine asked.

"The first vision saw her heading west," Ethan said with his firmly focused straight ahead, "The second vision saw where she ended up."

"Where?" said Katherine—mystified as to why they weren't moving yet. "Cecily could be in any of the small towns bordering the interstate. Which one did she go to? Monticello? Athens?"

Ethan shook his head and said softly, "Atlanta. She's in Atlanta."

Katherine sat back in her seat with a deep breath. "Atlanta?"

"Atlanta," he repeated a third time while his key still dangled in the switch.

"That's high queen territory," she said.

"Yes," Ethan confirmed. "I can understand if you want to stay here."

Katherine shook her head firmly. "If Atlanta's where Cecily is now, that's where we're going."

A small smile appeared on Ethan's face, then he cranked the engine.

Made in the USA
Lexington, KY
27 September 2014